NEXT VICTIM

Detective Rachel King Book 1

HELEN H. DURRANT

Published in paperback 2021
by Joffe Books, London
www.joffebooks.com

First published in Great Britain in 2019

© Helen H. Durrant

This book is a work of fiction. Names, characters, businesses, organisations, places and events are either the product of the author's imagination or are used fictitiously. Any resemblance to actual persons, living or dead, events or locales is entirely coincidental.

All rights reserved. No part of this publication may be reproduced, stored in retrieval system, copied in any form or by any means, electronic, mechanical, photocopying, recording or otherwise transmitted without written permission from the publisher. You must not circulate this book in any format.

ISBN: 978-1-78931-630-8

Printed and bound in the UK

For Melissa and Holly who spent, what for them was a boring and foot-aching day, wandering around the back streets of central Manchester while I did research and looked at locations.

PROLOGUE

Three years ago.

Alice Brough put the birth certificate on the table, smoothed it out and began to read, devouring every word. She'd spent long hours searching for this, and now she'd found it — her proof. Her twin brother was real. Not imaginary, like she'd been told so many times.

They seemed to think she'd made him up. "She needs other children to play with," her Aunt Hettie would say. She said this all the time. "It's no wonder she makes up fairy tales." Well, this would show them.

All the details on the certificate checked out. He had been born on the same date as her, fifteen years ago, to Julia and Alexander Brough, her parents. They'd named him Alfie. Alice and Alfie. Twins.

So, why the denial?

Well, there'd be no more uncertainty. She knew the truth now. Alice smiled. At last, the heavy burden of years of doubting had been swept away and her heart was lightened. She had a brother. His name was Alfie. He was no fairy tale but flesh and blood like her.

All she had to do now was find him.

But first she wanted an explanation, and that could only come from her father. Apart from him, what little family she'd had were gone. Aunt Hettie was in a home, slowly dying of dementia, and her mother . . . Alice couldn't remember what had happened to her. But she was long gone, and hadn't been mentioned in years.

Alice picked up the document and went to find her father. He was in the back garden, pruning his roses. Alice called to him from the French doors, waving the document at him. "Look! Come and see. Now you can stop telling me I'm mad."

For years, her questions about her brother had been dismissed as the ramblings of a lonely child. But Alice wasn't lonely. She clearly remembered Alfie, a real boy, flesh and blood, not some imaginary playmate. They'd played together in this garden, in this very house. Well, her father would have to come clean now. There was no denying the evidence in her hand.

Her father, Alex Brough, a tall man in his forties with a shock of prematurely grey hair, looked at Alice. What was he thinking? What was he remembering?

"Later, Alice. I've got to do this before it gets dark."

"No! Speak to me now. What do you know, Dad? What happened to little Alfie? What won't you tell me? Why?"

He swore under his breath and wiped his forehead with an earth-stained hand, leaving smudges of dirt on his face.

"He's not real, Alice. Alfie is in your imagination. I've told you."

"He is real, Dad. Look, here's his birth certificate." She held it up.

"You're mistaken. That will be for someone else." He looked at her, his expression exasperated. "I don't know what you want from me, Alice. I can't help you."

She almost stamped her foot. "The truth, Dad. That's all I want. Why all the pretence? What are you hiding?"

"Nothing. This has become an obsession, Alice. You must let it drop before it takes you over."

It was pointless arguing with him. Despite the proof in her hand, he was giving her the same old story.

"What about my mother, then? What happened to her?"

"She left us a long time ago. I've told you that too."

Another lie. Her mother would never leave her. "Did she take Alfie?"

"No. How many times do I have to say it? There *is* no Alfie, never was. Let it go, Alice. You'll make yourself ill."

Alice remembered her brother. She remembered the holiday they'd had on the south coast with Aunt Hettie that last summer. It had been real.

"I'm begging you, Alice. Accept that there is no Alfie and move on."

The problem was, Alice was not the accepting type.

CHAPTER ONE

Now — Sunday

The man took a deep breath. The air tasted sweet. It had been a satisfying kill. He closed his eyes and pictured his victim. Young, good-looking, perfect in fact. He'd picked him up in a gay bar on Manchester's famous Canal Street, and had arranged to meet him tonight outside another of the bars there. This wasn't a clever move, because there was probably CCTV. A mistake he'd avoid in future. Still, even if he'd been filmed with the young man on his arm, he was nothing but a nondescript shadow among the more flamboyant clientele that thronged the place.

At this time of night there was no one around this barren piece of land. Time to go before folk began staggering home from the bars and clubs. They used it as a shortcut. He slowly backtracked to the arch, his eyes on the ground. He was looking for anything that had been dropped, either by him or the lad. He also left certain items for the police to find. The plan he'd devised would tie the investigation in knots. The police would chase up the wrong suspects and, if he was lucky, charge them.

He hoped he'd been careful about forensics. He'd worn gloves and had made sure not to leave hair or anything else with his DNA on it at the scene. His and the boy's clothing would go in the garden incinerator.

Under the arch, he neatly packed the boy's clothes and his tools into his sports bag. He took a last look at the corner where he'd killed the lad, and a shiver ran up his spine. Now he could leave. Job done.

He strolled home, enjoying the cool night air, high on his success. He thought about the coming days. The media would be all over this in no time. The police would be forced to ask for their help. They'd have no identity for the boy and nothing that pointed to his killer. In the coming hours, the police would throw a fortune in resources into searching this area. But all they'd find is what he'd left for them, along with a few muddy footprints on the towpath.

He was in control.

He put his head down and his collar up in order to avoid being recognised on his way back to the train station. The worst thing would be if he met someone who knew him, always a possibility. He needed to blend in, to slip through the Saturday night crowds unnoticed, a nobody.

He'd taken his first victim tonight to test the plan. Now he could savour his success. Planning was key. He'd spotted him a few weeks ago, sitting outside his favourite pub on Canal Street, drinking a lager. The lad was a regular, always around at the same time. He was in his late teens, tall with a lithe body, obviously kept himself fit. The lad had longish, curly blond hair. This vision of beauty had been going around the tables, asking for money. When they first met the lad had said he was a rough sleeper, even better, unlikely anyone would come looking.

The man had called him over to his table and offered him a drink and something to eat. The lad had readily accepted, and the rest was a doddle. The man had gone over the scenario in his head numerous times, and hadn't expected to fail. They'd arranged to meet tonight. The man offered him money for sex, said he knew a place, and the lad had agreed at once.

He took off his gloves and put them in his overcoat pocket. He walked towards the lights of Oxford Road. Despite the late hour, there were people about, youngsters mostly, spilling onto the streets from the bars and clubs. He watched a young woman, skirt up to her backside, scream at her boyfriend. After treating him to a flurry of obscenities, she flounced off. Tut tut. A girl could get into serious trouble dressed like that in this area. Just as well he preferred young men.

CHAPTER TWO

Monday

Mornings in Rachel King's household were fraught. Escaping to another room with her coffee didn't help either. She could still hear the incessant bickering between her two daughters, Megan, eighteen, and Mia, fourteen. Why did this have to be the backdrop to breakfast every single day? Combined with the radio going full blast, it made for an uncomfortable start, to say the least. Today, the girls were at the kitchen table fighting over Megan's mobile. Mia had snatched it from her hands and was scrolling through the texts.

"Megan's got a boyfriend," Mia shouted.

Megan responded by cuffing her younger sister across the arm.

"Mum!" Mia cried. "She slapped me."

"Stop it, the pair of you. Eat up, or you'll miss the bus."

Rachel had had it. Mornings were hectic enough without all this. She couldn't hear herself think. Not wanting to get the day off to a bad start, she went outside into the garden and checked the messages on her own mobile. There was a rambling missive from her ex-husband, Alan, about the alterations to the house. He would have to wait.

The second one stopped Rachel in her tracks. Out of the blue, Jed McAteer had written wanting to know if she was free on Friday. She felt sick. How long had it been? Two years at least, she reckoned. That particular dalliance hadn't ended well, so badly, in fact, that Rachel had made a pact with herself. That was the last time. Jed was a bad habit she had to kick.

But she couldn't think about that now either, she had work to go to. Past mistakes would have to take a back seat. By now, the row between the two girls had escalated. Rachel could hear them out on the patio. The noise reached a crescendo just as the house phone rang.

"Shut it, the pair of you!" Rachel screamed, receiver in hand. Thankfully the call was from Elwyn Pryce, her detective sergeant. He knew what her life was like.

Rachel was a DCI with the serious crime squad for east Manchester CID, based in Ancoats. Currently she headed a three-person team. Given the growth of the area she'd been promised a DI, but that hadn't happened yet.

"We've got a body, ma'am, in Ancoats. A young man. It's a bad one. Looks like he was tortured, his throat cut, and then thrown into the canal."

Rachel felt her stomach lurch. *Not now. I can really do without it.* It had been a busy few weeks, and the team had hoped for some down time. Rachel looked at her girls. Noisy or not, she'd be lucky to see much of them for the foreseeable. "Text me the location. But it will take me at least thirty minutes to make it through the city at this time of the morning."

"The site is secure. Forensics and the photographers are on their way, and Dr Butterfield is already here."

Colin Butterfield was the home office pathologist. "Don't let him move the body until I've seen it." This was the part of the job that Rachel least relished, but it was necessary. She shouldn't have had to remind the pathologist about the body, but on the last two occasions, Doctor Butterfield had had it carted off before she arrived. Elwyn might be good at his job, but *she* needed to see the victim in situ.

Work call over, and the two girls were still going at it. She'd had enough. She snatched the mobile from Megan's hand. "Boyfriend? I thought we were supposed to talk. You tell us who he is and then we meet him. You know that."

"It's only Dan, Mum. She's being a drama queen as usual." Megan stuck her tongue out at her sister.

Mia folded her arms and turned away. "I've seen them kissing."

"You little snitch! You promised not to say anything."

"Stop that!" Rachel shouted. "Megan, you're older, you should know better. The pair of you, get ready for school — now! Mia, get your stuff from your room."

"I've got a tutorial," Megan said. "I'm meeting Alice at hers. We don't have to be at uni till eleven."

"Megan gets on my nerves." Mia bounded down the stairs, threw her schoolbag over her shoulder and took the money her mother held out for her. "Can't take a joke, that's her problem."

"I can still hear you," Megan shouted from the kitchen.

"If you're so fond of this Dan, bring him home, Meggy. Let's give him the once-over."

"Mum! He'd hate that."

"Okay, but don't blame your sister for telling. I need to know what's going on in your life. It's for your own good, you know. It's a tough world out there." Rachel kissed Mia's cheek. "It's your dad's for tea tonight, and don't forget. Off you go, or you'll miss the bus."

Rachel's marriage had survived till Mia was ten. It had fallen apart after she'd got her promotion to DCI. She'd been thrilled at the promotion, but the extra responsibility and increased workload was the final straw for her relationship. Once she was engrossed in a case, everything else took second place. All the apologies in the world couldn't make up for the missed family events and school plays. When she'd had to miss Christmas the year Mia turned nine, Alan had flipped.

She couldn't blame him, and in a way, it was a relief. Rachel was fond of Alan, she loved him after a fashion, but not in the way a wife or lover should. She'd settled for second best and had carried the guilt for a long time. The man she really wanted, the one she'd been in love with since her teens was Jed McAteer.

Thinking back to those uncomplicated times brought a smile to her face. They'd been neighbours in the student accommodation block. Rachel was at college because of her ambition to work in the police force, but for Jed, it was simply a way of leaving home. Despite having the entry qualifications, Jed McAteer was no student, but he was good-looking. The fact that he'd fallen for her too had Rachel counting her blessings. He could take his pick.

Rachel was tall and slim, her eldest described her as 'willowy'. Facially she had good bone structure, framed by curly red hair which grew fast and had been the bane of her life in her teens. Rachel harboured no illusions. She was attractive, but her nose was a little long and she made little effort on the makeup front. Fashion was another alien land. Jeans and a shirt, with a warm coat and boots in winter would do.

Rachel fell for Jed almost at once and he for her. They spent every spare minute together. Then Jed fell in with the wrong crowd. Rachel would despair at his antics, but she never imagined that it would have the outcome it did.

During the first year of their studies, Jed was arrested and convicted of handling drugs. He did a short spell in prison and that sealed his fate. Despite her love for him, any further relationship was out of the question because of Rachel's burning ambition to be a detective. It was a straightforward choice, her career or Jed. She chose her career. A decision vindicated when Jed returned to a life of crime on his release. University over, Rachel fulfilled her ambition and joined the police. At that point she put all thoughts of Jed out of her mind. It hadn't been easy, but eventually she met Alan. She tried very hard to make the relationship with him work. But kids aside, settling for Alan had been a mistake. The divorce was payback for Rachel.

Alan knew none of this. Rachel had let him believe that the split was entirely down to her job and the pressure it put her under. It was kinder that way, and it suited both of them in the long run. Alan was a good man and determined to do what he could to ensure that their daughters didn't suffer. He knew the strain she was under. The kids plus a demanding job was a plateful in anybody's book. They had talked it through and had agreed to share responsibility for the girls. But what Alan did next surprised them all. He bought the house next door. A great help as far as child care went, but a little daunting to have your ex privy to all the minutiae of your life.

Alan was an architect and worked mostly from home. It was a blessing, and Rachel didn't knock it. He did demand a certain amount of quiet time away from the kids when he was busy or seeing a client, but on the whole, he was very accommodating.

After one last look, she deleted the text from Jed McAteer. She checked Alan's again. He'd arranged for a builder to come and look at the properties. He'd been going on for months about wanting to link the two semi-detached cottages by building a sunroom that would join them together at the back and overlook the gardens. The idea was that the girls could come and go freely. They had discussed it, but Rachel hadn't paid much attention. Now she read that Alan had produced the drawings and wanted an estimate for the work. The only positive Rachel could see at the moment was that it would provide the girls with a space of their own.

The house phone rang again. This time it was Detective Superintendent Stuart Harding, Rachel's immediate boss. What the hell did he want? Like she didn't know. Checking up on her was his favourite pastime.

"I'm surprised I caught you," he said.

This was Harding-speak for *what are you doing home at this time of the morning?* No good arguing. In his book, Harding was always right

"The canal killing." He wasn't one to waste energy on idle chitchat. "I want you as SIO on this one, and we need a quick result. We haven't had a good press of late and we need to redress the balance, regain public confidence." There was a pause. "I'm relying on you, DCI King. Get down there at once and don't let me down."

"We'll do our best as usual, sir," she said. "If that's all, I should get going."

CHAPTER THREE

DCI Rachel King donned a white coverall, overshoes and gloves and pulled the hood over her curly red hair, carefully tucking in a few wayward strands. The usual scene played out in front of her. The forensic team were spread out over the area, heads down, faces intent. The photographers had made it before her and were busy snapping the body from every angle.

The pathologist, Dr Colin Butterfield, was examining the victim, and Rachel went up to him. He was a man in his fifties, tall and slim with thinning hair and a ruddy complexion. DS Elwyn Pryce was bent over at his side, taking in everything that was said. She trusted this quietly spoken Welshman, who worked closely with her. They were friends as well as colleagues.

DC Jonny Farrell was the newest member of the team and the youngest, a sharp dresser. He stood with his hands in his coverall pockets, shifting his feet and trying not to look like a spare part. Every few seconds he glanced down at his shoes. As she got closer, Rachel saw the look of distaste on his face and smiled to herself. The mud and filth of the canal bank had seeped over the elastic of the plastic overshoes and was no doubt staining the expensive leather.

"I'd say dead since last night," Butterfield called up to her. "But I'll know more after the post-mortem. Naked. Several deep lacerations to the head and body, and the throat cut. Butchered, you might say." He grimaced. "Luckily he hasn't been in the water long."

"Luckily? I don't think our victim would agree with that," she said.

Rachel hadn't seen one as bad as this for a long time. Parts of his body were so badly burned that both the epidermis and dermis had split, allowing the fat beneath to melt and leak out. He was young, probably no more than twenty. He lay on his back, and his eyes — lifeless black smudges — stared up at nothing. He was tall and skinny. All that remained of his hair was the odd blond wisp sticking up from a bloodied scalp. But apart from a few scratches, the skin on his face was smooth, untouched. It was an angelic face, and made him look younger than he probably was. The only blemish on it was a mole, high on one cheekbone.

"The burns are patchy. Parts of his torso and his face aren't damaged at all. In other areas, he looks like he's been fried," Elwyn Pryce said.

"It's difficult to say how the burns were inflicted," Butterfield added. "But even though he's been in the water, I can still detect the faint whiff of petrol."

"Did the burns kill him?" asked Elwyn.

"I'll tell you that after the PM. But if they didn't, the cut on his throat certainly did. It's right around, and deep. He'd have bled out in no time. It's a good clean job too."

Rachel swallowed hard. "Thorough job, then."

"Yes, and he took his time."

She nodded at the body. "Who would want to do that to another human being?"

"A nutter? Some mad bastard?" Jonny Farrell offered.

"That isn't helpful, Jonny," Rachel said. "Was he conscious?"

Butterfield shrugged. "Difficult to say. We'll do a toxicology screen. With luck, he was drugged. But if the burns didn't kill him, once his throat was cut it would have been quick, that's for sure."

If the burns were inflicted first, death would have been a welcome release. The lad had suffered. The burning would have hurt like hell. Rachel consoled herself with the thought that he would probably have lost consciousness by then. The pain would have been excruciating. At least fifty percent of the surface area of his body was an ugly, raw wound. Rachel leaned in for a closer look. It looked like he'd fallen into a vat of boiling water.

"Who called it in?" she asked.

Elwyn Pryce shook his head. "Some male, and that's all we know. He didn't give a name. I've already checked, and the phone was an unregistered pay-as-you-go."

"Obviously got something to hide. We need to find him." Rachel turned her attention to Butterfield. "Is there anything that might give us an ID?"

Butterfield shook his head. "Not that I've seen so far. No clothes, watch, nothing. It will be down to forensics or luck to sort that one."

"Our killer went to a lot of trouble. He might have wanted something from him. Money, information, who knows?" Elwyn said.

"What is this place?" Rachel circled around, trying to get her bearings. They were on a large tract of waste ground dotted with piles of rubble, with the canal running through it. The waterway would run from here up into the city, and back to the Bridgewater in the other direction.

"The railway still uses some of the buildings you see over there in the distance. Those mills to the right have been empty for donkey's years. I read in the paper that this entire area is earmarked for renewal, but I won't hold my breath," DC Jonny Farrell said. "The homeless use those arches under the railway line to sleep in, and gays bring their pick-ups from Canal Street here." He sniggered. "Makes me queasy, just thinking about it."

Rachel threw him a questioning look. Jonny was new to the job and young. Some aspects of what they dealt with embarrassed him. On the surface he was streetwise, but he had a lot to learn about human behaviour.

"Is this what happened here, I wonder? Any sign of recent sexual activity?" she asked Butterfield.

"Difficult to tell, might be impossible. You'll have to wait until I get him on the slab."

Fair enough. "Come on, Jonny, bring a torch and let's go explore. Make sure you get plenty of photographs," she called over her shoulder.

Rachel walked across to the row of arches with Jonny reluctantly trailing behind her, cursing as his feet sank into the mud.

"Most of these are boarded up but one or two look accessible. That one over there." Rachel pointed. "The train tracks run overhead and the tramline is on the far side as it rolls into Piccadilly. Scream as loud as you like, I doubt you'd be heard."

"Given the burns on his body, there'd be a lot of screaming." Jonny shuddered. "You don't think he was killed on the towpath then?"

"He's been beaten, burned and had his throat cut, so no, I don't."

The two of them stepped into the dark interior. The concrete floor was strewn with rubbish and a pungent smell of rotting food and urine permeated the air.

Jonny screwed up his face. "What a bloody awful place. To think, the homeless use these holes to sleep in. Poor buggers."

But Rachel wasn't thinking of the smell. What they could see was more important. Her eyes darted about, taking in every dark corner. This was the place, she just knew it. And Rachel's gut instinct was rarely wrong.

"See? Here, on the floor. It's black, sooty," Rachel ran her gloved hand lightly over the mark. "And that over there, on the floor — blood splatters." She weighed up the chances of being seen or heard from the outside. Minimal. "Get the victim in here and the killer would have had plenty of time to do his worst. I think this is the kill site. It's a long shot, but I wonder if there were any homeless around last night? Any idea how we might find out?"

"I'll have a word with the organisation that provides food. There's a group that goes around handing out sandwiches and hot drinks."

"Do that," she said. There was plenty for the forensic team to go on here, but would they find anything to help identify the killer, or even the victim come to that? She hoped so, otherwise they were stuffed.

"There's a pile of rope here on the floor, and all sorts of rubbish stacked in that corner. What d'you think, ma'am?"

"I think this is the place where the young man was tortured. Once his attacker had done his worst, he carried or dragged him out to the canal to dump him." Rachel stood up. "Get forensics to go over this place thoroughly. There is a slight chance we might get some DNA."

"If our victim was brought here for a quick fumble, they could have met up the road on Canal Street," Jonny suggested. "It's only a few hundred metres away."

"We'll make enquiries, check out the CCTV and speak to bar staff. But first, we need to know exactly what happened to the young man. The post-mortem will give us some answers." She looked at Jonny. As yet, he hadn't been keen on the gorier side of the job. "Do you want in?"

He made a face. "Okay . . . But if I puke, please don't tell the others."

Rachel nodded. Let him keep his credibility intact.

Suddenly she grabbed his arm, pointed to a passageway that led through to the neighbouring arch and gestured for him to be quiet. "There's someone in there," she whispered. "Don't let him get by." With Jonny following, she stepped into the dark passageway.

"I didn't do 'owt! I didn't see 'owt neither."

An elderly man, bent double and apparently in pain, emerged from the shadows. "I didn't kill the lad. I've never harmed no one."

He wore a filthy ripped overcoat with a long scarf wrapped several times around his neck.

"It was you who rang us?" Rachel asked. It was a good guess.

The man nodded.

"Did you sleep here last night?" she asked.

He nodded again, took a step forward, lost his balance and crashed into Jonny.

"Ma'am!" the young detective gasped, "he's off his head. He stinks of whisky."

"We'll take him back to the station, give him a bite to eat and let him sober up. Then we'll see what he has to say."

CHAPTER FOUR

Rachel tapped the photo pinned to the incident board. "The PM is scheduled to take place within the hour. Me and Jonny will attend." She looked at DC Amy Metcalfe, the other woman on her team. "Amy? The guest we brought in from the scene is still sleeping it off. If he wakes up before we return, give him some food and keep him happy. We need his help. He was in those arches last night, and he probably saw or heard something."

DC Amy Metcalfe stuck up her arm, and Rachel nodded at her, hoping for a useful contribution for once. It was about time Amy pulled her weight.

Amy was thirty-one, Rachel thirty-nine. Not a great deal of difference, but unlike Rachel, Amy had no children in her life, and no man either. She had expensively cut chin-length blonde hair and was never seen without her makeup. Rachel couldn't imagine where she found the time. Most mornings, it was all Rachel could do to brush her hair. Off duty, Amy was something of a party animal, and this morning she obviously had a mammoth hangover. Her three or four strong coffees and the paracetamol she kept popping were a dead giveaway.

"Ma'am, I've checked missing persons. So far no one matching the victim's description has been reported," Amy said.

"If the lad was a rough sleeper, that's what I'd expect. We don't know how long he'd been living on the streets, so you'll have to go back further."

Amy pulled a face, annoying Rachel. So the DC didn't enjoy rummaging around in records. Who did? When she was on form, Amy had the makings of a good detective, but she needed to sharpen up. She was rather too careless about her work and often made mistakes. And unlike Rachel, she seemed to have no feel for the job, no gut instinct. Her mediocre notebook was her only weapon in the fight against crime.

"The CCTV from Canal Street should be in," Rachel said. "It's a stab in the dark because all we have is the photo of the lad taken at the crime scene, and he doesn't have much hair in that. But he was blond and he has a distinctive mole on his cheek. Take a look, and see if you can spot him. We'll meet back here early afternoon. See what we've got."

Her mobile beeped, and she checked it quickly. It was a second text from Jed McAteer.

I won't take no for an answer. Dinner, Friday. We deserve some you and me time.

Rachel almost dropped the phone. When they parted for the last time, they'd decided that contact wasn't on. It caused too much upset all round. He knew the score, so why was he being such a persistent bugger all of a sudden?

"Problem?" Elwyn asked.

"No, just the kids," she said. "Want to know what's for tea."

"They're big enough to fend for themselves, surely?"

"They're lazy, Elwyn. Lazy to the core. If I don't feed them, God knows what they'll be eating."

Elwyn Pryce was the only member of the team who Rachel spoke to about her family. Personal issues, and homelife, were all best left on the doorstep each morning. It saved complications. But Rachel was only human, and sometimes she needed someone to offload to. The quietly spoken Welshman was a friend. They'd been working together for years now, and she trusted him not to gossip. But she wasn't daft. The others would be well aware of her circumstances — the divorce, her daughters' antics. They'd have overheard her talking to Elwyn, and ranting at Alan over the phone.

She was in two minds as to what to do about Jed. Should she ring or text him, remind him of what they'd agreed? Or perhaps it would be best to ignore him and hope he got tired of bothering her. But why now? It worried Rachel. She hoped to God he wasn't connected with the new case.

"Jonny, get your gear. We're off, and you can drive." She'd negotiated the city traffic once today, and didn't fancy a re-run.

* * *

The morgue was attached to Manchester Infirmary on Oxford Road. The forensic labs were housed in a purpose-built facility a few hundred metres away.

Colin Butterfield was gowned up and ready for them. In the ante-room, a technician handed the two detectives their coveralls. Rachel didn't like this part of the job, to put it mildly, and she knew today's PM would be one of the worst. Through an adjoining glass door, they could see the victim laid out on a trolley, his body covered by a white sheet.

"Ready?" Butterfield asked as soon as they entered the room. The technician removed the sheet, and they turned their attention to the young man laid out before them.

"I have already had a look at the body and made some preliminary notes. Our victim is tall, underweight for his age. The condition of the body means that I can't say for certain whether there was any recent sexual activity. Death was caused by severing of the carotid artery when his throat was cut. He'll have bled out fast. That, and all the other cuts on his body are clean and precise. The blade was thin and sharp. You're looking at a scalpel or one of those DIY knives." He leaned in closer. "It was a clean job."

"Was he drugged?" Rachel asked.

"Tests are ongoing to see what drugs are in his system."

Given the extensive burns and the state of him, Rachel hoped they'd find a whole shed load, otherwise the lad would have suffered horribly.

"Prior to death, the lad was beaten. His bottom lip is split open and there's a tooth missing. I cannot determine if there is other bruising because the skin is so burnt. However, prior to his chest being mutilated, two of his ribs were broken."

"What about the burns?" Jonny asked.

"Inflicted before death. He lost a lot of blood, which indicates that his heart was still beating when his throat was cut."

"Any idea how he got burnt?" Jonny asked.

"Difficult to say, but as you can see, the burning is in patches. We have sent skin swabs off to the lab. Despite him having been in the water, there was a smell of petrol when we were on the canal bank. The burns are far worse in some areas than in others."

"Are you saying he had petrol poured over him?" Rachel asked, horrified.

"Not poured, exactly. Possibly the fluid was wiped over his body and then set alight."

This wasn't going well. They needed something to work with. "Have you ever seen anything similar?" Rachel said.

"No. I've seen plenty of burned bodies, but none quite like this. More tests are required, I'm afraid. I'm not in the habit of guessing. Like you, Detective, I deal in facts. Best wait until the lab results are back." Butterfield took his knife and made the customary incisions down and across the body. Jonny looked away.

"He hadn't eaten much in a while. Stomach contents consist of the remains of what looks like a cheese sandwich, and lager."

That would match with him having been on Canal Street prior to his death.

Butterfield removed the internal organs from the body. He examined each one and sloshed them into a bowl. Rachel cast a glance Jonny's way. He was pretty green, but doing a good job of holding it together.

"Rough sleeper? What do you think?" she asked.

"The burning makes it difficult to tell," Butterfield said. "Ordinarily, with a rough sleeper you'd expect the feet to be dirty, and the teeth not cleaned for a while. Given the extent of the burning, and the muddy canal bank, that doesn't apply. There is debris under his fingernails but again, that could come from where he was found."

Rachel sighed. They needed more if they were to find out who he was.

"I may have found something." Butterfield was wiping the grime from the soles of the young man's feet. "He has a tattoo, here on the right arch."

"What is it?" Rachel asked.

"Not an image as one might expect, but a word." Butterfield took a magnifying glass and examined it carefully. "A name, in fact." He smiled.

"C'mon then," Rachel said. "Don't keep us waiting. What's the name?"

"Alfie."

CHAPTER FIVE

Back in the incident room, Rachel addressed the team. "We may have a name for our victim. He has 'Alfie' tattooed on the sole of his right foot, on the arch to be precise. That needs research. Contact the tattoo parlours. It's an odd place to have one, so someone might remember."

Rachel was not in the best of moods. Although she wasn't squeamish, post-mortems still upset her. They gave her an uncomfortable feeling in the pit of her stomach. Brought home all the horror of the inevitability of death. A year after her divorce, Rachel had lost both her parents in a car crash. As their only child, she'd had to identify the bodies herself. Their faces were imprinted on her memory. The two people she most loved, staring up at nothing with empty, sunken eyes. The image would stay with her forever. These days, she couldn't enter a morgue without remembering those faces. It was particularly poignant just now, because it was almost the anniversary of their deaths.

"Have we heard anything from forensics?" she asked, shaking her head to rid herself of the memory.

"Yes, ma'am," Jonny said. "Apparently they found a number of interesting objects at the scene."

"Objects? What objects?"

"A number of nuts and bolts."

Rachel shrugged. "They are significant how?"

"According to one of the forensic bods, it's like someone removed gloves or a cloth from a pocket, for example, and they fell out. They may have been dropped by the killer. So far forensics have recovered a dozen or so, all picked up between where the body was found and the kill site."

"That area was covered in debris. I don't see what makes these items so significant."

"They are new, ma'am. They hadn't yet become soiled from mud or the weather. That means they hadn't been there long."

Rachel turned to the rest of the team. "Any ideas?"

"There's a small industrial estate a few hundred metres further on from the scene and on the other side of the canal. One of the firms there deals in bolts," DS Elwyn Pryce said.

"You and me will pay them a visit." This could lead somewhere. Right now, it was just what they needed. "What about our guest? How's he doing?" The elderly rough sleeper was a witness. He had important information which might help.

"Last I looked, he was snoring his head off," Amy said. "D'you want me to get a uniform to wake him up?"

"No. Just keep an eye on him for the time-being. If he does wake, be gentle with him. If we are to get anything from him, he's got to trust us. We want the man's help, remember."

"You don't think he's our killer?" Jonny asked.

"Did you take a good look at him?" she said.

"Sort of."

"Well I did. He's old, small, thin, and riddled with rheumatism. Give him a push and he'd drop like a stone. I doubt he'd have the strength to do what was done to that lad."

"There was a call for you earlier, ma'am," Amy said. "Someone called Adrian Percival."

Rachel nodded, knowing who this was. It was nothing to do with the case. Ade was the builder Alan used. He'd want to know when it was convenient to visit the house. She'd text him later. She said nothing to the others.

"Anything from the CCTV?" she asked.

Amy and Elwyn both shook their heads.

"Amy, you and Jonny carry on while we're out," Rachel said. "I want movement on this. And don't forget the tattoo parlours. I'd like an ID at the very least, soon. The poor lad could have family out there somewhere."

"The super showed his face earlier," Elwyn said.

"What did he want?"

"Looking for you, I presume. Stuck his head around your office door and then left."

Rachel groaned inwardly. The last thing she wanted right now was a conversation with Detective Superintendent Stuart Harding. He was hard work, and she wasn't in the mood. "He'll want an update. I bet the press are clamouring. If we have nothing at the end of the day, a statement and possibly an appeal might be on the cards."

"Do you want a word before we leave?" Elwyn said.

"No, I don't. In fact, let's get out of here before he comes back."

The two of them took the stairs. "I'll drive," Elwyn said. "Why not get yourself a coffee from the machine?" There was one in the entrance.

She smiled at him. "You don't have to mollycoddle me, you know."

"I don't know about that, Rachel. You're looking a bit ropey these days."

"Thanks a million. Right confidence booster you are!" She laughed. But he was right. She caught a glimpse of her reflection in the glass front of the machine. She looked tired, pale and thinner in the face. Not just in the face either. Her clothes were looser around the waist and hips. Missed meals and lack of sleep did that. Not to mention worrying about why Jed McAteer suddenly wanted back in her life. She ran her fingers through her curly red hair. It was cut to chin length, and complimented her deep blue eyes. Well, normally it did, but now, with her pallor, it simply made her look peaky.

Elwyn looked at her. "I do know what month it is."

The anniversary of her parent's death. Like she needed reminding. She sighed. "Everyone else in my family seems to have swerved it, whether that's deliberate or not, I can't tell. The actual day is next Monday. I haven't said anything to the girls. Both of them are so wrapped up in their own lives, and I don't want them upset."

"What about Alan?"

"I doubt he'll remember either. He has a new project. He's planning on joining our two houses together." She laughed. "God knows what's going on inside that head of his."

"Wants you back. Plain as the nose on your face."

"Do one, Pryce. Been there, done that and don't want a repeat performance, if it's all the same."

"My parents are off to Spain for a couple of months. That means their cottage in Rhos on Sea is empty. You have time owing. If you want to get away, it's yours."

"Thanks, but I couldn't. There's the case for a start. The girls have school and uni and won't leave their mates, and I couldn't go alone."

It was kind of Elwyn to offer. He was a good friend and did his best to look out for her. In another life, they might have been close. Elwyn was easy to get on with and he wasn't bad-looking, still lean, and with a full head of dark hair. At forty-four, he was only a few years older than her. He was married, to Marie, but they had no kids. As far as Rachel knew, they were happy. He never said otherwise.

"Might do you good. North Wales. Get some reasonable weather, and the place is glorious."

"Thanks, Elwyn, but I'm a lost cause at the moment. I'm no good for anyone, not even myself. Work is the only thing that'll get me through the next couple of weeks."

CHAPTER SIX

It was time. The house was empty and he was alone. He'd retrieved the lad's stuff from the shed, and with the incinerator ready to go, the man was all set.

He wore rubber gloves. His victim had been a rough sleeper. His clothing was old and dirty, no doubt sourced from charity shops. There were enough of them about. Problem was, touching it could play havoc with personal hygiene. He could pick up anything from this little lot. But it was satisfying work. Each item he retrieved from the bag took him back to a moment of intense enjoyment. The lad had been a beauty. A blond, smooth skinned, godlike creature. Just like the one from his past, the lad seemed to radiate innocence. But the man knew the truth. He knew that the lad's heart was filled with hate. He needed to be got rid of, and it had been easy. A few words, a smile, and the die was cast.

One by one he threw the items into the incinerator. Underwear, socks and trainers. His nose wrinkled in distaste as he handled the lad's jeans. They were heavily soiled and smelled bad.

How he had enjoyed pulling them from those long legs! He closed his eyes. He could see the lad now, lying there, limp, naked, helpless.

Get a grip. She'll be back any time. She can't find you in this state!

He shook himself back into the here and now. There'd be time for memories. Now he must get this over and done with. All trace of the lad must be got rid of. He smiled, proud of what he'd done. It was testament to his ability to formulate a plan and for it to work perfectly, right down to the last detail. And there was more to come.

The lad had been his first kill. An unsuspecting victim, who was only too willing to do the man's bidding for money. The man had often seen the lad on Canal Street and had come to know his habits. He wondered if the police had found the items he'd left behind, and if so, what they'd made of them. They would soon discover where they'd come from, and then there'd be questions, interviews. It was the only lead the police had, so they'd be thorough. Served the pompous old bugger right. He was another man from the past he ached to get even with.

The clothes were rapidly turning into a pile of ash. Shame, he was enjoying reliving the act. Inflicting the horrific burns had been the final touch, and the most satisfying. His final victim must suffer the same fate — the burning was the whole point. He would scream, and then know just what he'd done. But he had to get it right. The man had expected the boy to shriek and beg for mercy, but he hadn't. He'd caused him too much pain, and it had made him pass out. That, plus the Rohypnol, liberally laced with diazepam that he'd put in his lager. Next time, he wouldn't make that mistake. The pain was a big part of the fun. He'd have to measure it out carefully if he was to get the right effect.

Nearly done. Only the lad's jacket to go now. The thing was old, soiled, and he went through the pockets gingerly. He'd no idea who the lad was, and at the time he'd not wanted to know. He'd said his name was Alfie, but that was probably a lie. Now it was all over, he was curious. The pockets were empty apart from some cash, a debit card and a student identity pass in the inside pocket. Not expected given the lad was living rough.

The student ID card had the lad's image on it, and his full name. The man had been right, it wasn't Alfie. It was unlikely he was a rough sleeper either. He'd been a student studying journalism at Manchester University. So why pretend otherwise, what was his game? Suddenly an alarm bell rang in his head. Where was the lad's mobile? He went through the pockets again. Nothing. Had it been in the jeans?

Think, man, think. It was important. That phone was vital evidence. He took a metal bar and started to rake through the ashes. There was no way of knowing for sure whether it had been burned. He closed his eyes. He would have to chance to luck. It was too late to do anything else. But then it struck him. Why not try ringing the number? See what happened. But if it was already in the hands of the police, they might trace him.

He sat down in a garden chair. Worst case, the police had it. They'd look at the calls and texts, nothing to incriminate him there. But there were fingerprints, even DNA, to consider. But his weren't on file. There was no way the police could trace that mobile back to him. Relax, he told himself. You're safe. The police might not have it anyway.

The clothing was soon consumed by the flames. Gone. All that remained were the memories of this, his first kill. Now he craved more. High on his first success, he had an urgent need to line up his next victim. Hanging around the gay bars waiting to spot a likely candidate was risky. He didn't want people to start recognising him. So, last night he had registered on a gay dating site using a fake profile. From now on, his prey would be chosen with more care.

"You still at it?" The familiar voice rang out from the back door.

She was home. He had to be quick before she wanted to see what he was up to.

"Coming, sweetie," he said. "Just getting rid of some rubbish."

CHAPTER SEVEN

Paul Greyson, the owner and manager of Greyson's Hardware, showed Rachel and Elwyn into his office. The walls were lined with wooden filing cabinets and a huge oak desk dominated the room. Rachel glanced at the photos, but all showed men in suits shaking hands with Greyson. Business associates, not family. The single window looked out over the yard.

They introduced themselves, and Rachel got straight to the point. "We're investigating the murder of a young man that took place sometime last night. He was found only a few hundred metres away from your warehouse."

"Got nowt to do wi' us, love. I know what types use the arches over yon. We keep well away."

Paul Greyson was a big man. He didn't so much talk as bellow. Rachel could imagine the workforce cringing at his every word.

Elwyn showed him his phone with the image of the nuts and bolts. "Do you manufacture these?"

Paul Greyson shook his head. "We don't manufacture anything. We import all our stock and sell it on to our customers." He took a catalogue from his desk and passed it over to him. "All the items we carry are in here."

"It's quite a range," Rachel commented, looking over Elwyn's shoulder. "You have a warehouse and staff?"

"Yes. I've currently got ten warehouse staff, plus Mrs Andrews in the office, a nightwatchman and my three drivers."

"But can you confirm that this is your stock?" Elwyn enlarged the image of one of the bolts.

"Aye. It's come from here, alright. See that stamp there?" He pointed to a set of numbers on the image. "That particular bolt, and thousands like them, was delivered last week from a firm in China we deal with."

"Talk us through what happens when stock arrives, Mr Greyson," Rachel said.

"I'm sorry, Miss," he looked Rachel up and down, "but I don't see where this is getting us. I'm a busy man with clients to see. This is wasting both your time and mine. The folk who work here had nowt to do with any murder."

"We'll be the judge of that, Mr Greyson," Rachel said. "How can you be so sure anyway?"

"Because it's dead simple. The lorry with the stuff arrives out there in the yard, we unload and then the staff store it away. When we get orders in, we generally use our own transport, but if that isn't feasible we use a carrier."

"You're sure that nothing leaves your buildings unless it's for a customer? Boxes don't get dropped or disposed of, out there for example? The nuts and bolts that were found are small. They could have been left at the bottom of a box." She nodded at the tract of waste ground in front of them.

"No way. We dispose of our rubbish properly. They might only be small items but we deal in bulk. Some of the country's largest companies are our customers. Can you imagine if we were found to be illegally dumping rubbish? A lot of our customers would stop dealing with us."

"Do your staff ever help themselves?"

"No. It'd be the sack if they did, and they know it."

Greyson was obviously getting annoyed with this line of questioning. "You heard about the body that was found in the canal?" Rachel asked.

He nodded. "It were on t'news."

"Can you offer any explanation as to why some of your stock might be found at the scene?" she said.

Greyson's face turned red and he loosened his tie. He was no doubt wondering where these questions were going, and not liking it. This man must rule his little empire with an iron fist. He wasn't used to anyone doubting his word.

"You've got it wrong! They weren't from here. No way!"

"But, Mr Greyson, you've just identified them as coming from your stock," Rachel said.

"I don't know what you're trying to prove, young lady, but it won't work with me. No one here has murdered anyone. There must be some mistake."

"This wasn't the only nut and bolt we found. There were six in total," she said. "Since you haven't offered me a reasonable explanation, we're going to have to interview your staff. They'll need to provide alibis for last night. You too."

"Nonsense! All this fuss for half a dozen nuts and bolts! You've got this all wrong. None of the stock leaves here unless it's part of a consignment." He was shouting now.

"We're investigating a murder, Mr Greyson. Pieces of your hardware were found at the murder scene. Unless you can offer me an explanation, we must investigate."

"Have you had a break-in recently?" Elwyn asked.

"No. I have good security, a watchman and CCTV."

"We'll need to look at that too," Rachel said.

"You're making a huge mistake. No one here had anything to do with any murder. Who was killed anyway?"

"We don't have a name yet," Elwyn said.

"Well, you'll get nothing from us. We can't help. You can have the CCTV and access to my staff but don't expect anything. They've been with me a while, and all provided good references. I don't see any of them being a killer."

"You're probably right, but we do have to follow it up. I'm sure you can see that. If you could give us the CCTV, we'll be on our way." Rachel forced a smile.

"Leave me your email address. When Mrs Andrews comes back from her break, I'll get her to send you the web address and password. We use cloud storage for our CCTV."

They went back to the car.

"What d'you think?" Elwyn asked.

"Tricky. He's one of those men who think they are always right. That's his domain in there. Everyone does as they're told, and no one dare put a foot wrong. We come along and put it to him that one of his workforce could be involved in a murder. Sent him spinning well out of his comfort zone, that."

CHAPTER EIGHT

Amy was grinning like the cat that had got the cream. "We've spotted him, ma'am. One of the bars at the end of the street. The CCTV is positioned so that it takes in a few of the tables outside. Our victim's going from one table to another. It looks like he's asking for money. He appears to do quite well. One or two even hand over notes."

"Are you sure it's him? The victim was in a pretty bad way."

"It's the shape of the face, ma'am. I'm sure it's our victim."

Amy had paused the film at a particular frame. Rachel and Elwyn moved closer to have a look.

"That does look like him," Rachel said, recalling what she'd seen of the victim. "He's untidy. Those clothes don't fit properly. His hair looks like it hasn't been cut in a while. He certainly looks like a rough sleeper."

"He puts the money in his jacket pocket," Amy said.

"We've no jacket. No clothes at all in fact. Anything could have happened to the cash. The killer may have taken it. For now, I'm more interested in who he speaks to. Does he sit down with anyone?"

"Not that we can see, ma'am. In all the shots he appears in, he's moving. Unfortunately the other cameras on the street are looking in the wrong direction."

Ah well. Nothing Rachel could do about it. "Thanks, Amy. Good work."

"DCI King, do you have a moment?"

It was Detective Superintendent Stuart Harding. He'd come in while everyone's attention was on the screen.

"Certainly, sir." Rachel led the way into her office. Harding looked drawn and tired. Something was bothering him. Hopefully it wasn't just the current case. She wanted him off their backs.

"Do you have an identity for the victim yet?"

"No, sir."

"In that case we'll do an appeal. I'll arrange for a press briefing later. You and I will take the stage. We'll put out a photo and answer general questions only. You have a suitable image of the young man, a description they can use?"

"Yes. We have a good shot of him on CCTV taken on the day he was killed."

"Good. We need a decent response. A murder victim, and still no ID." He shook his head. "It doesn't sit well. The public expect more."

"Needless to say, we are doing our best. We are following several leads. I feel confident that with or without the appeal we'll have an ID soon."

"Not guaranteed. Not unless he's reported missing."

"There are aspects to the case that make me think otherwise, sir. There's a tattoo on his foot, for example. It's a name, possibly his, and it's in an odd position. We're checking the parlours."

"An appeal will yield results faster."

"Is that all, sir?" Rachel knew from his demeanour, the reddening face, the straight back, that Stuart Harding was holding his true feelings in check. He had a temper which he found difficult to control. It seemed to be getting worse. Lately, his expectations of his teams had become almost impossible to achieve.

"Keep me informed, understand? I want an update on progress daily. I'll let you know when the briefing is taking place, but it will have to be tomorrow now." He turned on his heel and marched out.

"He looked edgy," Elwyn said.

"And the rest. He wants to put out an appeal. It might give us something, but more than likely we'll end up with a load of timewasters." Rachel looked around the incident room. The team were heads down at their desks. "Amy, our guest in the cells. Have you spoken to him yet?"

"He's been asleep all day, ma'am. He was shattered. He woke briefly, had a cuppa and then went off again."

"Make sure he's checked regularly. We don't know his medical history. I don't want him keeling over with some condition we know nothing about." She turned to Jonny. "The tattoo parlours. Anything?"

"I'm still going through them, ma'am," he said.

Rachel went back into her office. It was gone six in the evening and she needed to speak to the girls, make sure everything was OK. She sat at her desk and took her mobile from her bag.

"Meggy, you with your dad?" Megan grunted. "Is Mia home? Has she taken her meds?"

Mia had type one diabetes and needed regular medication. It had been under control for nearly three years now, and Rachel wanted it to stay that way.

"For God's sake, Mum. We're all fine," Megan barked. "I'm trying to work and I've got a deadline!"

"Try being me!"

"It's not all about you, Mum. I'm doing a degree, remember? Mia's had her injection and gone round to Ella's. Some panic on about homework. When will you be back?"

"I could be late. Don't wait up. Best if you and Mia stay at your dad's tonight. Keep an eye on your sister. Don't let her stay up until the death."

"He's had that bloke round about the extension," Megan said. "It sounds pretty cool. We'll be able to come and go as we want between the two houses."

"Yeah, well cool!" Rachel snorted. She'd no idea what was really going on in Alan's mind, but this was an expense they didn't need.

There was a knock on her office door, and Jonny Farrell barged in. "I've got something!" He beamed at her.

CHAPTER NINE

"A bloke who runs a tattoo parlour in Fallowfield remembers the lad," Jonny said excitedly. "He went into the shop with another boy and a girl. The tattooist reckons they were students. He thought the request odd, both in terms of where he wanted the thing, and the name. Apparently, his real name wasn't Alfie."

"Does he know what his name was?" Rachel asked.

"No. When the work was done, the girl paid with her debit card. The bloke did say he got the impression it was some sort of joke the group intended to play on a mate."

"We need that debit card record," Rachel said. "Students. Local, did he think?"

"He didn't say, but it's more than likely. We've got enough colleges around here."

And that was the problem. "Get the debit card info from the bank first thing in the morning and we'll go from there. We find the girl who paid, and we should have the identity of our victim," Rachel said.

Amy stuck her head around the door. "Uniform have been on. Our guest is awake and asking to be released."

"In that case, we'd better have a word. He should certainly be well rested by now, and sober. We won't get a better time." It was gone seven, and the team had been hard at it all day. "Amy, you can join me. Elwyn and Jonny, get off home."

Rachel saw the look Amy threw her way. She wasn't happy. Had she been planning another night out? What it must be like to have no ties! "He needs a gentle touch. He's more likely to talk to us women," Rachel explained. "I don't want him to see this as an interrogation."

"No probs, ma'am. I wasn't doing anything this evening anyway."

Rachel caught the sarcasm. She watched Amy rummage around in her desk and retrieve her mobile.

"A quick call and I'm ready."

Amy went off into the corridor to make her call. Rachel shook her head. If Amy had had something planned for tonight, she should have said so. She wasn't a bloody mind reader.

The old man had been asleep for hours. God knows when he'd last washed or changed his clothes, because he stank to high heaven.

Rachel took a sheet of paper from the uniformed officer. The man had given his name as John Jones.

She smiled at him. "Are you feeling better, Mr Jones?"

"Can I go now, love? I've got places to be."

"We've got one or two questions first. You were in the arches last night when that young man was murdered. It would help if you could tell us what you remember. We want his killer found."

"I didn't see 'owt." He stared at Rachel. His face was filthy with ingrained dirt. "It were too dark, and I'd had a bit to drink." He looked down at his hands. They were shaking, Rachel noted. "I heard him screaming though. Cut me to the quick. Poor soul, that beast hurt him bad."

"Yes, we know that. Did you hear anything else? Any names, for instance?"

"No. I think he were drugged. He were out of it for most of the time, to be honest. But whoever killed him were a cruel bastard. Kept hitting him. And if that wasn't enough, he took petrol and burnt him . . . I've never seen the like of it."

As Butterfield had thought. Rachel would get that information to him as soon as she could. She saw Amy wince. "You said *he*. It was definitely a man? Did you see him?"

"No, not really. He were in one of them all over white suits and a black coat, and I only saw him from the back. Even his head were covered. I suppose it could have been a woman, at a pinch. I don't hear too clear, and what with the booze an' all, I can't be sure. But he had a torch that lit the place up a bit. I could see the boy were in a bad way. He must have been heavily drugged because he screamed a bit, but he should have made a lot more noise than he did."

"You're being very helpful, John," Amy said. "You phoned us too, that was a good move."

"It were his phone, the lad's. Not mine."

Rachel looked at Amy. "What happened to it?"

"The custody sergeant will have it."

"Arrange for it to go to forensics. We should be able to get the call log."

"Will you let us help you now, John?" Rachel asked. "Perhaps get you a place in a hostel? I could make a call on your behalf."

"Hate them places. No, love, I'm fine on me own. Can I go now?"

"We will need to contact you again. There is every chance you'll be called as a witness once the case goes to court."

"I've a brother in Ashton, Pennington Court flats, number eight. He'll get a message to me."

Amy had been writing down everything John Jones had told them. "Would you mind signing this before you leave?"

"Can't write. Never learned." He put a huge cross at the bottom of the paper, and then stood up.

"See him out, Amy, and get him a hot drink and a sandwich from the canteen before he leaves." Rachel left the room with some relief. The smell was making her feel queasy. She didn't understand why he'd refused her offer of help.

CHAPTER TEN

For more than an hour, he sat hunched over his computer, squinting at images of young, blond men. He didn't want to pick just any young blond man. He was looking for a particular type. It had been easy with 'Alfie,' he'd spotted the likeness at once. But finding the next one might not be so straightforward.

For various reasons, he'd disregarded most of them and was now left with two. Both were local. Good, it meant less travelling. And both bore a resemblance to victim number one.

It was never his intention for there to be only one victim. These young men were practice for something far more important. And he would keep on practising until he got it right. His cold, dark eyes flicked rapidly from one face to the other as he tried to decide which one to go for.

In the end, he chose a youth with golden curls and a cherubic face. They had to be like that, there was a very good reason for it. It too was part of the quest.

The young man called himself 'Luke.' Wondering if that was his real name, the man sent 'Luke' a message, calling himself 'James.'

Earlier that evening, he'd taken a walk down Canal Street and sussed out the cameras and where they were pointing.

He'd identified an outside table where they wouldn't be recorded. That would be the meeting place. All he had to do now was set it up.

He wrote, *I am looking at your profile. You are beautiful. I am captivated. Please agree to meet me. You will not be disappointed.* A click, and the words went off into cyberspace.

Several minutes passed with no response. The man grew anxious. Had he come on too strong? Or perhaps Luke wasn't online.

I am free tomorrow, Tuesday evening.

The man smiled. This was too easy.

The next message read, *I want to look at you, can we facetime?*

Not possible. He'd put a photo on the dating site but it had been heavily photoshopped in an effort to disguise himself. He'd added a short beard and moustache and dyed his hair a shade darker. He planned to do this for real before meeting his date in person. He'd already let his facial hair grow.

Can't. Wrong sort of phone. Don't worry, I'm like you, just a guy looking to meet up with someone I can trust. Meet me tomorrow, Canal Street at seven. You can make up your mind then. If you don't like me, I'll understand. I will be sitting at an outside table, wearing a rose in my lapel.

A bit old-fashioned, but what was wrong with that? Again he waited. Did the young man suspect that something was wrong? Was he having second thoughts? He hoped not. Now the man had settled on Luke, he was keen to firm things up.

Yes, I'll be there.

Arrangements made, Luke signed off. The man was pleased at his success. Things were looking good, but he must go carefully. This time he wouldn't rush things. 'Luke' would be reeled in slower than the last one. There were still some loose ends to tidy up.

The man took the student identity card from the breast pocket of his shirt. His first victim had been studying at Manchester Metropolitan University. He accessed Facebook, logged in using his fake account and typed in the name on the card. It took a few minutes, but finally he found him.

A pretty face in a halo of flowing blond hair. Seeing the profile photo brought it all back — the anticipation, the thrill of the slow kill. The pain and the helpless victim's reaction.

The lad had been twenty, a student from Stockport in the second year of a degree course. He had two parents still alive, no siblings and hundreds of friends. In his spare time, he enjoyed football and going to concerts. Didn't they all?

One photo showed him surrounded by a group of girls. Did they know he was gay? One of them, a pretty girl with long, blonde hair was kissing his cheek. The man found her name — Hayley Burton. He smiled to himself. Was Hayley missing him? There had been nothing on the news. That meant his first victim had not yet been officially identified.

Enough. Going over it again wouldn't satisfy his need for long. The man was now gazing at a different Facebook profile. This one was familiar. It belonged to someone he used to know well, someone he hated with every fibre of his being. That hate was what drove the man forward, what led him to kill. He had to get even, take revenge for what that person had done to him.

The man often checked this particular profile. He was older now, his golden curls long gone, and the angelic face bore the lines of a life that hadn't been easy. Served the bastard right. The man on the Facebook profile stared back at him, a cheesy grin on his face. Who was he kidding?

"Hello there, long time no see," the man whispered, lightly touching the image. Time had not been kind to the face beneath his fingers, and that pleased him. It was justice of a sort.

"Have you missed me? Ever wonder what happened? Where I went? You won't have to wonder much longer. I'm going to put you straight. Be warned, your world is about to change. I am coming for you."

CHAPTER ELEVEN

Tuesday

For once, the house was blissfully quiet. No arguments, no stamping up the stairs, a rare peaceful start for Rachel. The girls were next door with their dad. The weather was kind too, a sunny late April day that promised more warmth than they'd had in a while. What to wear? Rachel settled for jeans and a shirt. If Harding put in an appearance, she kept one of her good jackets in her office.

Several cups of tea, a couple of slices of toast and she was ready for the off. Her mobile beeped. It made her jump. Jed again? She hoped not. Relief, it was a text from Alan. He was taking the girls to a restaurant in town so she could forget about dinner. She sent back a smiley emoji. Alan was worth his weight in gold at times.

Another beep, more nerves, but this time it was Elwyn. They had a name for the woman who'd paid for the tattoo, Hayley Burton. Her current address was a student house in Fallowfield. That made sense, given where they'd got the tattoo done.

It was progress. Elwyn would get the address and text it to Rachel. The girl must know who the young man was. Then they'd have an identity, and the case could move forward.

Rachel lived several miles out of the city in the village of Poynton, not far from Macclesfield. When she'd split from Alan, she'd bought two semi-detached stone cottages with the idea of knocking them together. That had never happened. Time, money and the job meant her plans were constantly put on hold. In the end she'd had no choice but to put the cottage they didn't use on the market. Not ideal, Rachel wanted the space for the kids, but it was the only choice given her circumstances. It sold almost immediately — to Alan. Her first thought was, would he ever give up? And that she would have appreciated a discussion. At the very least to have been told! Had she been aware of what he planned to do, Rachel would have made him look elsewhere. She objected to having Alan spy on her every movement, question the late nights and general slog that came with the job. But as it turned out, it was a blessing. It solved all her childcare problems, and Alan was able to keep a close eye on Mia.

A major drawback of living so far out was the traffic. Today's journey seemed to take ages until, finally, she hit the A6. From there she crawled with the rest of the traffic as far as the traffic lights in the centre of Fallowfield. Here, she swung a left onto Grange Road. Her satnav indicated that she wanted the next turning on the right.

It was a cul-de-sac of large Edwardian houses. At one time, these would have been worth a packet, but they had long since been bought up by investors and converted into student accommodation. Each house no doubt brought in a decent amount in rent, having ten or more rooms with a communal sitting room and kitchen.

Elwyn met her at the door. "I've rung the bell but no one's responded."

Rachel checked her watch. It was gone nine. "They could have left for uni, I suppose. Try again."

Elwyn hammered on the door. Nothing. He tried a window. Finally, a young woman flung open the front door. She was wearing a dressing gown, and her hair was wet.

"Where's the bloody fire? I was in the shower. What do you want?"

"We're police, love." Rachel showed her badge. "Is Hayley Burton in?"

Rachel saw the doubtful look. The girl was considering her response.

"Look, I'm late. I've got to leave soon. Why do you want her, anyway?"

"Is she here or not?" Rachel was running out of patience.

"Come in."

The girl led the way inside. The place was untidy, with empty cans of lager and festering take-out cartons strewn about. The girl brushed some rubbish off the sofa and nodded for them to sit.

"I'm Hayley," she admitted. "But I've done nothing wrong — as far as I know."

"We're not saying you have." Rachel assured her, still on her feet. There was no way she was sitting down in here. "We simply want a chat. We think you have some vital information about a case we're investigating. You paid for a young man to have a tattoo done in a local parlour, isn't that right? On his foot."

Hayley grinned. "That's right. Alfie."

This girl could have vital information, Rachel decided to risk the arm of the settee. She handed Hayley an image of the lad, taken from the CCTV on Canal Street. "Who is he?"

"Ollie," she said at once. "The tatt was a joke. He isn't really called Alfie."

"Oliver who?" Elwyn asked, notebook open.

"Oliver Frodsham. He's at college, like the rest of us. Why? What's he done? We're not in trouble over the joke, are we? We were just winding Alice up — that's Alice Brough. After he had the tatt done, Ollie spent about two weeks pretending to be her long-lost twin brother. I realise it was a bit stupid, but we were drunk and Ollie wasn't bothered, he was well up for it."

"Why would you do that to Alice? Surely you realised how upset she'd be once she discovered the truth?"

"We didn't think," Hayley shrugged.

"Why Alfie and not some other name?" Rachel knew very well the answer to that one, but wanted to hear what the girl had to say.

"Like I said, it was a joke. A way to wind up Alice. She's so intense, so into finding this long-lost brother of hers. She drives everyone wild with her constant going on. We just wanted a way to make it stop." She thought for a moment or two. "But I think Ollie had other ideas all along. He saw Alice as a soft touch and intended to get what he could out of her. You see Alice has money, and now I think that's what Ollie was really after. And he did very well out of it. Alice took him home, gave him money. I have no idea how much, but I bet that stupid tattoo was well worth it."

"When was the last time you saw Oliver?" Rachel asked.

"About four days ago. He stayed here, dossed down on that sofa." She smiled. "He's a bit of a loose cannon, is Ollie. Sometimes we see a lot of him and then he'll disappear for days on end. He's doing a journalism course, always chasing some story. He was full of himself when he came round here. Working on a story about the homeless in Manchester. Said the story was dynamite. Said if he got it right, there'd be big money in it, and he could dump college. He also told us that some big-time villain had hired him to keep watch on a piece of land, note and report on who came and went."

Rachel's stomach lurched. "Did he give you the name of this big-time villain? Say anything else about it?" She waited for the reply, praying the girl didn't say it was McAteer.

"No idea. He didn't tell us much."

"D'you know why the land was so important?" Elwyn asked.

Hayley shrugged. "No idea, but he really got into it. Pretended to be one of the rough sleepers so he could doss down nearby. That way he reckoned no one would take much notice of him."

"Do you know where Oliver came from? Anything about his family?"

Hayley began to look worried. "Something's happened, or you wouldn't be here. Has he had an accident, got himself into bother? He's not been arrested, has he?"

"No, not arrested." Rachel told her gently. She couldn't say anything further until a family member officially confirmed that the body was Oliver Frodsham's.

The girl sat down. "He is in bother. I can see it in your faces."

"We can't say too much until we've spoken to his family."

"They live in Heaton Norris. It's not far. Just carry on up the A6, through Stockport and beyond."

"We know where it is," Elwyn said.

"Do you know his address?" Rachel asked.

Hayley shook her head. "It never came up."

Rachel smiled, trying to look reassuring. "Ollie's friends. Are they students like you?"

"Ollie knew a lot of people, but yeah, they're mostly students."

"Would you write down as many names as you can remember, please? We'll need to speak to them."

Hayley took the notebook and pen Rachel offered her and scribbled away for several minutes before handing it back.

"Thanks. You've been a great help. We'll be in touch." Rachel said, getting to her feet with some relief. "Here is my card in case anything occurs to you that you think we should know."

They went back to the cars. "She turned out to be quite helpful in the end," Elwyn said.

But Rachel was staring at the list of names. "My Megan is on here. She must have known him."

CHAPTER TWELVE

"If Oliver's friends prove to be important witnesses, you can't interview Megan," Elwyn said.

"I know that, but first things first. We've still got to confirm the lad's identity and tell his parents."

"Has Megan mentioned him? Said anything about him being missing or about the murder?"

"No, Elwyn. At least, I don't think so. But then I've not seen much of the kids. I've been too busy."

This was an important lead, but Rachel's head was too full of other stuff for her to think straight. She had a bad feeling. Hayley said she thought Frodsham was working for some villain. If that was Jed McAteer, she was stuffed. It was no secret that he was one of Manchester's most infamous crime barons, but what no one knew was that he'd once been the love of her life. Once. Who was she kidding? Even today she was still susceptible. She had to keep away from him. Their relationship was a secret, and Rachel was prepared to move heaven and earth to keep it that way, her career depended upon it. Was it just coincidence that he'd been texting her these last couple of days? Or did she have a problem?

There was no time to dwell on this now. Rachel rang the office and spoke to Amy. "Get on to the uni and find out the home address for an Oliver Frodsham. It will be in Heaton Norris somewhere. When you've got it, text me. We're on our way."

"They're students," Elwyn was saying, "they see each other around. Megan probably didn't know him that well."

"I think she might have done." Rachel sighed. "This Alice Brough that Hayley was on about. She's close to Meggy, has been since they first started. Alice lives within walking distance of us, and she sort of latched onto her. They got the same bus into uni, and they became friends."

"You know her?"

"Not well, but she's been to ours a few times. She's eaten with us occasionally. She's an odd sort, Alice. She wears weird clothes and does her hair in old-fashioned styles. To look at, her and Meggy are poles apart. But they get on, and they are both on the same business course."

"An individualist, then?"

"Very much so."

He nudged her. "Your phone's beeping."

It was Amy, sending her Oliver's address. Rachel tapped the postcode into the satnav and then passed it to Elwyn. "Let's get this over with."

Elwyn followed Rachel's car to the address and parked up behind her.

"I hate this part of the job, Rachel," he said as they surveyed the property. "I don't have kids of my own, but it's still the hardest thing in the world to tell parents their child has been murdered."

"I wonder what they're like, his family? They probably think he's safe at uni, doing his thing, getting the grades. When I say goodbye to Meggy in the mornings, I don't for one minute imagine she's sloping off somewhere else. But it seems that young Oliver was."

"His parents will have to ID the body." Elwyn grimaced.

"Don't worry, they won't see what was done to him," Rachel said. "I hope they kept in touch. We need to know a lot more about that young man's life. This story he was after sounds interesting, a motive for his murder perhaps. Who knows what he'd stumbled on?"

Her mobile beeped, making her jump. Her nerves were getting the better of her. This had better not be Jed again.

"Problem?" Elwyn asked. "Is it Mia?"

"No." Relieved, she said, "My running club is putting together a contingent for the Manchester marathon. They want to know if I'm in."

"Don't know how you can. Where do you get the energy?"

"I have a demanding job, mad kids, one of whom has a condition, and an ex who won't let go. Believe it not, I don't always sleep nights. Late at night, when everyone's finally asleep, going for a run clears my head."

"I find a couple of whiskies does it for me." Elwyn smiled.

The house was a modern detached one in a new development. He whistled. "Money."

"Let's get on with it." As they walked up the drive, Rachel saw a woman watching them from the front window. "This bit always makes me nervous. You never know how they're going to take it." She rang the doorbell, steeling herself.

A middle-aged woman answered the door.

"Mrs Frodsham?" Rachel said.

"Yes. It's Ollie, isn't it?"

Rachel could see at once that this woman had spent sleepless nights worrying about her son. She probably knew a little about his life, but not the bits that mattered.

"I've been ringing him constantly and getting no reply. That isn't like him. We speak, or he texts me, several times a week. Not about much, mostly about his coursework. To be honest, I've picked up the phone to ring the police several times, but I haven't been able to go through with it."

"Can we come in?" Elwyn asked.

"What's he done? Is he hurt?"

"We'd like to speak to you, ask you some questions, if we may," Rachel said gently. "Is there anyone with you?"

"My sister. We were about to go out. Come inside."

A second woman was standing in the doorway of the kitchen.

"Sandra," the woman said, "the police are here. It's about Ollie."

As they walked the length of the hallway, Rachel glanced at the numerous family photos on the walls. One captured her attention straight away, and she paused. It showed a young man whose blue eyes seemed to follow her. A blond lad with a pretty face and a mole high on his cheekbone. There was no doubting it now. Ollie was their victim.

CHAPTER THIRTEEN

Rachel stood at the front of the main office, ready to address the team. The room was full — her own people along with several uniformed officers who would help with the legwork. She'd had a difficult lunchtime. Another brush with the dead.

"Earlier today, I accompanied Mrs Frodsham, our victim's mother, to the morgue." Her voice faltered. She cleared her throat. This wasn't like her. Rachel had to learn to do this job without becoming prey to her emotions every time she dealt with something difficult. But the reality was heart-wrenching. Rachel had had to stand by and watch a woman, not much older than her, being confronted with her dead son. She watched her break down at the loss of the most precious person in her life. Throughout Sheila Frodsham's ordeal, Rachel had thought of her own daughters, and how she'd feel if it were one of them lying there in the morgue.

"She has officially identified the body as her son," Rachel said. "Oliver was twenty. He was studying journalism and media at Manchester Met. He contacted his mother several times a week, but he chose not to live at home. There is adequate public transport into the city from Heaton Norris. His mum didn't question this, putting it down to him wanting his privacy."

"What about his dad?" Jonny asked. "Where was he?"

"Oliver's parents are divorced. His father pays for the house and keeps the pair of them. He has a job in IT and travels extensively for work. He rarely sees either of them."

"Did Oliver have a permanent address?" Elwyn asked.

"He gave his mum the address of a friend at the student house in Fallowfield we visited. When Oliver first started his course, he gave his mum a fake address. We have no idea where he actually stayed or why he did that. Once he got to know other people at uni, he seems to have spent his life sofa surfing."

"Seems an odd thing to do when he'd a perfectly good home a few miles away," Jonny said.

"Does his mum know what might have got him killed?" Amy asked.

"We didn't go there," Rachel said. "It's too soon. She was too upset. We'll speak to his uni friends first, see what they have to say. One of them, Hayley Burton, told us he was hired by some villain to watch a piece of land, although she'd no idea why. That's an important line that needs following up. I'm hoping that one of his fellow students will give us a clue."

"It's possible he trod on someone's toes. I'm thinking of the gay angle. Perhaps he simply picked up a wrong 'un and paid the price," Jonny suggested.

"We certainly need to know a lot more about his personal life. Who he dated, and who his friends were outside college. But we'll start with what we've got and wait for forensics." Rachel looked up. Stuart Harding had entered unnoticed and was standing at the back of the room. "We have an ID, sir," she said. "It might be an idea to hold back on the appeal."

"Frodsham?" He said thoughtfully spotting the name on the incident board. "I know a Graham Frodsham. Used to play golf with him."

"Probably coincidence, sir." Rachel smiled, hoping that's all it was. She turned her attention back to the team.

"Specific points of action. Amy, get onto the university. Arrange for us to meet with Oliver's friends, and the people on his course. Preferably today. You and I, Elwyn, will go see what we can find out. Jonny, take a walk down Canal Street and speak to the people who work in the bars. Take a photo with you, see what they know about Oliver."

"You're not sending our pretty boy down there, surely, ma'am? They'll have him for dinner." Amy sniggered.

Rachel frowned at her. "Leave it out, DC Metcalfe. This is a serious business."

"Will you tell his friends what's happened?" Jonny asked, and glared at Amy, his face red.

"Just the basics, no gory details. Their friend has been murdered, that'll do for now."

"Ma'am, the lad's phone records are in," Elwyn said. "It was a cheap pay-as-you-go smartphone, but he'd taken several photos." The DC had them up on his computer screen. "The quality isn't bad. They're mostly of the small industrial estate the other side of the canal. And of Greyson's in particular."

"Why Greyson's?" Rachel circled the name on the board. "Coupled with finding the nuts and bolts, that firm has suddenly become a great deal more interesting. Interviewing the staff there is now a priority."

"DCI King," Harding called out. "Keep me informed. Any significant developments, I want to know at once."

Harding left. Rachel took a deep breath. She knew what he wanted, a quick result. But a case like this had to take as long as it needed. Meticulous investigations and forensics would get them there in the end.

"Is there anything from the lab yet?" she asked Jonny.

"They're still doing tests, but they've confirmed that he was a drug user. They found traces of cocaine in his blood."

"We need to find out who his supplier was, and if he owed money for dope. Cross the wrong people, and that's another way of ending up dead in the cut."

"His student friends might know. He's turning out to be quite a boy, our Ollie." Jonny smiled.

"He was young, living away from home for the first time. He upset someone, that's for sure, but don't be too quick to judge him."

"Sorry, ma'am, just saying."

"We have several strands to look at. First, we speak to his fellow students at college. After that, Elwyn and I will investigate the Greyson's connection. Amy, once you've arranged for us to see Oliver's friends, find out who he made those calls to."

CHAPTER FOURTEEN

The entrance to the university, on Oxford Road, was crowded with students. Rachel and Elwyn had to elbow their way into the building. It brought back Rachel's student days. She and Jed had both studied at UCLAN, and they spent every spare second together. She closed her eyes for a second. Why did her mind do this to her? Why did she have to keep thinking about Jed?

"Oliver's course tutor has organised a room for us," Elwyn told Rachel. "It's on the fifth floor. Walk, or take the lift?"

Rachel smiled. "You know I don't do lifts."

Rachel's phobia about lifts dated back to the early days of her marriage to Alan. The pair had gone to a Victorian hotel on the east Yorkshire coast for their honeymoon. The place had a lift that was practically a museum piece. Ramshackle and shaky, it had a grill which you had to push aside before you opened the doors. The lift was so small there was only room for one inside, and that terrified her. As Rachel told Alan, it was nothing more than a vertical coffin. Then what she'd been dreading happened, she became trapped between floors, alone and in the dark. It took hours for the engineers to release her. A terrifying experience which she never wanted to repeat. Ever since then, she'd mistrusted lifts, and took the stairs whenever she could.

"C'mon then — race you!"

Bad move on Elwyn's part. She was much fitter than him. By the time they reached the fifth floor, he was gasping. "You need to get back in training," Rachel said smugly.

Elwyn was bent double, his hands on his knees, taking in gulps of air. "I . . . let you beat me," he panted. "You're the boss and I want a favour."

"Work favour?"

"No, personal."

That sounded like trouble. "We'll talk later," she said hastily. In a room at the end of the corridor, Rachel could see groups of teenagers sitting around the tables. "This lot'll take some sorting."

Rachel and Elwyn walked in. All eyes turned to look at them, and the chatter suddenly ceased. They'd obviously heard about Oliver.

"I'm DCI King and this is DS Pryce. We want to speak to you all about Oliver Frodsham," Rachel began.

A tall woman stood up. "I'm Pam Reed, one of Oliver's lecturers. Talk to the students by all means, but I'll sit in if you don't mind."

"Is it true he's been murdered?" asked a blonde girl.

"Yes." A silence ensued, followed by a few stifled mutterings. "You were his friends," Rachel continued, "and there are things about Oliver's life that we need to know if we are going to catch his killer. We're hoping you will help us."

There was more murmuring around the room and then the blonde girl stood up.

"People thought Ollie was friendly, the get-on-with-anybody sort, but he was more complicated than that. I think he was in trouble. He stayed a couple of nights at ours and didn't want anyone to know where he was."

"What sort of trouble?" Elwyn asked.

"Someone was looking for him. He wouldn't say who, just that the man was dangerous. Ollie was secretive. We were his friends, yet he didn't trust us. For instance, he dropped out of his course but he wouldn't tell anyone why. I don't think his mum knew either."

"Can you think of a reason why?" asked Rachel.

"Ollie wanted to be a journalist. He was always working on some story or other. And he'd recently become involved with a local businessman, a developer I think, and some villain. I got the impression something dodgy was going on, but Ollie wouldn't say. I think he was threatened. I guess he had more to be scared of than we realised."

First a villain, now a local businessman and land. Rachel's nerves sounded another warning. Jed was a crook but in recent years he'd also turned developer, no doubt as a cover for his more nefarious dealings. But he was successful, and responsible for a number of housing estates that had sprung up around the city. It gave him a veneer of respectability.

"What's your name?" Rachel asked.

"Grace Hopton," said the girl.

"Does anyone else want to add anything to what Grace has told us?" There was a general shaking of heads. "Okay, but my colleague and I will still have to speak to you all individually."

"You can use the office next door." Grace pointed to it, and they went through.

"What d'you think?" Elwyn asked Rachel once they were inside the small office.

"I think we get set up and start rolling them through. There must be a couple of dozen out there. If we don't watch out, we'll be here all night."

"A local businessman, eh. Greyson?" Elwyn said.

"Don't jump to conclusions. We need a lot more."

"Can I be first?" The voice came from the doorway.

Rachel looked up and recognised Hayley from the student house in Fallowfield. "Do you have something you want to tell us?"

Hayley Burton sat down. She looked nervous, and was biting her bottom lip.

"Have you spoken to Alice?" she said.

"Alice Brough?" The girl nodded. Alice was Megan's friend. "Not yet, but we will."

"Alice hated Ollie. I mean really hated him," she said. "That joke with the tattoo that Ollie and some of us played on her? Given how she felt about finding her brother, she took it badly. Swore she'd get even, and that Ollie would rue the day. How were we to know she took the thing about her brother that seriously? To be honest, some of us doubted he ever existed."

Rachel looked at Elwyn. Was he thinking the same as her? A joke taken too far? A motive for murder, perhaps?

"When did you last see them together?"

"A week or so ago, when Alice found out the truth. She was furious, even went for him with a knife in the canteen. Mr Gaskell, one of the lecturers, had to stop her. She was practically foaming at the mouth. I had no idea she had such a temper."

Neither had Rachel. The Alice she knew was a gentle soul who loved animals and was a committed vegan. She would never have imagined that sweet girl as being capable of violence.

"Alice lives at home with her dad, but he's often away. She has freedom and enough money to do what she wants. Ollie was staying there before they fell out," Hayley said.

"Has Alice said anything since you learned about his murder?" asked Elwyn.

"She's not been in. That's strange too. I don't recall her missing any lectures since we started the course."

"Thank you, Hayley. That was very helpful."

CHAPTER FIFTEEN

The two detectives were on their way back to the station.

"What now?" Elwyn asked after a long silence.

"Alice appears to have a motive," Rachel said. "Harboured a grudge perhaps, but I don't see her as a killer."

"Nevertheless, we'll have to interview her about what happened." Elwyn said.

Rachel shook her head. "It took strength to do what was done to Oliver. Dragging him to the canal bank wouldn't have been easy either. Alice is a tiny thing, skinny. I want to know about that scoop Oliver was after, and who it involved. He may have trodden on someone's toes and suffered the consequences."

"Hayley said Alice had money," Elwyn said. "Perhaps she got someone to do the killing for her."

"I don't see that either. I doubt Alice knows anyone that dodgy. Let's not get bogged down with the Alice angle."

"The scoop Oliver was after then. Perhaps he crossed one of this city's real bad guys."

God, she hoped it wasn't Jed. The idea that the young man could have crossed the villain made her feel sick. Jed did not forgive, he got even. If it came to it, there was no way she could interview him. What excuse could she make to Harding?

"Where career criminals are concerned," she said, "swift and to the point is the usual choice. Execution is what they do, with a bullet or a knife. Our killer went to a helluva lot of trouble, took his time. Not what we're used to with gangland killings."

Elwyn was doubtful. "It could still be, Rachel, despite not fitting the profile."

"Well, we've no idea, have we really? All we know is that Oliver Frodsham upset someone. That someone could've been Greyson or Alice. Then again it could be someone we know nothing about. Some villain wanting revenge, for instance."

If this was down to one of the first two, they were in with a chance. That would please Harding. If not, they could be chasing their tails for months. No one had ever gotten anything on Jed McAteer, if that's who Oliver was afraid of. Plenty had tried, but the man was too clever, and he had plenty of people to watch his back.

She decided to change the subject before Elwyn mentioned any names she'd prefer not to hear. "What's the favour then?" she asked. His face clouded over. "C'mon, something's up, I can sense it."

Finally, he blurted out, "Can I leave some of my stuff at yours?"

"What sort of stuff? Not junk, I hope. Can't you just bung it in the garage like most folk?"

"It's my personal stuff — books, photos and some clothes."

"Clothes?" She stared at him. "Elwyn, what's going on? How do you square this with Marie?"

"I don't, and she won't give a damn anyway. I'm leaving her. The marriage is over."

Rachel was gobsmacked. Elwyn and Marie married young, in their late teens. Everyone thought they were the perfect couple. She wanted to ask what had gone wrong, but bit her tongue. This wasn't the time. They must be good at hiding the truth. She'd only seen them socially a fortnight ago, and all had appeared well.

"I'm sorry. I had no idea."

"Made my mind up last week, actually. I'd reached the stage where I knew I'd had enough. We don't love each other anymore, that's all there is to it. There's no one else, unless you count the job." He gave her an awkward smile.

Rachel understood only too well how he felt. She'd never really loved Alan. She cared for him, loved him as a friend, but that was as far as it went. The job had filled a void in her life too. Jed McAteer had been the man she wanted. She'd been smitten ever since her teens and had never got over it. But it wasn't to be. As soon as she found out what he was, she'd dumped him. It broke her heart, but what else could she do? If she wanted to keep her sanity — and her job — Jed had to go.

"You can have the study. None of us uses it. The girls do their homework in their rooms and I use it as a dumping ground anyway." She heaved a sigh. "That puts paid to Boxing Day nights round at yours. What will we do now?"

"You can still come. We're still friends, you and me."

"Not the same though, is it? I enjoy my chats with Marie. Over the years, the job has put paid to a lot of girly friendships. They got fed up of inviting me out and being let down."

"It's coming to something if me and Marie are the sum total of your social life," he said with a smile.

"That's about the size of it."

"Thanks, Rachel, I owe you one. I'll come round later if that's okay with you."

* * *

As soon as they entered the incident room, Rachel asked Amy, "Oliver's phone records, what have you got?"

"He sent several text messages and made a number of calls during the few days before he was killed. To just four numbers. He never contacted anyone else using that phone. One of those numbers belongs to Alice Brough. I'm still investigating the others."

"Did Alice text him back?"

"Boy, did she! Rants on about that tattoo and him making a fool of her, and how he wouldn't get away with it." Amy held out the transcript.

The words were harsh, Alice promising to get even, make him pay. Given that the lad was murdered, they'd have to take the threats seriously. "The other numbers — is one of them Greyson's by any chance?"

"Not their main number. It might be Greyson's personal mobile, I suppose. I'm still working on it."

Rachel had no time for this. "Give it here." There was a quicker way to find out. She tapped the number into the office phone and rang it. "Mr Greyson," she said, beaming at the team, "we need another word with you. My colleague and I will be round within the hour."

The look she gave Amy said it all. The sergeant needed to sharpen up. "Has anyone looked at the CCTV from Greyson's?" No one replied. "Well, come on. I can't do everything myself. Get it accessed and start ploughing through it."

Rachel left them and went into her office. She needed coffee and to check in with the girls. It would be another late one. Not that she minded, Alan was sorting the meal, and she'd grab a sandwich for herself later.

Elwyn Pryce stuck his head round her door. "Want me to come with you?"

"Okay. We still need to speak to Alice Brough. Greyson first, then Alice. After that we'll call it a day."

"Don't forget what I said about my stuff," Elwyn said.

"You're sure about this? I help you out and people might see it as me condoning your breakup, which I don't," she added swiftly. "You and Marie have always been the perfect couple."

He shook his head. "Not anymore."

Rachel picked up her mobile and rang Megan. She wanted a word about Alice. "Where are you, love?"

"At home. Restaurant's off, Dad's got a client coming round. He's asked me to order pizza or something."

"Have you seen Alice today?"

"She rang me earlier. She's not well. I was going to pop round later, try and cheer her up."

"Don't!" Rachel insisted. "We're going to speak to her about Oliver Frodsham's death, so I want you to keep away."

"You can't be serious, Mum. Alice won't be involved. Her and Ollie were okay. You've got this horribly wrong."

"It's just a chat, but stay away until I tell you different."

There was a knock at the door. Amy. "Ma'am, you should see this. We've found something."

"Don't forget what I've said, Meggy. Keep away."

Rachel could only hope that her daughter did as she was told for once. Alice obviously had a violent streak that she didn't want Meggy falling foul of.

The film was as clear as day. Oliver Frodsham and Paul Greyson, arguing in Greyson's yard. It was just a pity that there wasn't any sound.

"That's not all." Amy smiled. "Later on, when the place is closed up, Oliver comes back and climbs over the fence."

Rachel studied the few seconds of film closely. What was going on? Greyson wasn't stupid. He must have realised they'd see this when he'd given them access to the film.

"Amy, take a couple of uniformed officers and bring him in. He's got some explaining to do."

CHAPTER SIXTEEN

Paul Greyson was not a happy man. "This is outrageous! What am I supposed to have done?"

They were in an interview room at the station. Greyson was sitting opposite Rachel and Elwyn, with the duty solicitor beside him.

"Mr Greyson, we have a few questions for you about the murder close to your premises," Rachel began.

"I've already told you. That had nowt to do with us."

"We now have a film clearly showing the victim in your yard. If you would take a look, please?" Rachel handed him a still taken from the CCTV.

Greyson's eyes narrowed. "This is him, is it? Never seen him before. Can I go now?"

Rachel sat back in her chair and folded her arms. She was going to enjoy watching him wriggle out of this one. "I'm wondering why you're lying to us, Mr Greyson."

"I'm not in the habit of lying, young lady. Now, charge me with something or let me go."

"Do you know where we got this photo?"

"Not a clue."

"From your CCTV. Now how do you explain that one?" Rachel took a series of still images from a folder and set them down one by one in front of Greyson. They showed the progression of the argument between him and Oliver, up to the moment where Greyson was shaking his fist at him.

"It's a fit-up." Greyson cast a sidelong look at the silent solicitor.

"Film doesn't lie, Mr Greyson. You obviously did know the victim, so why not just say so? What aren't you telling us? What have you got to hide? Perhaps we should start again." She tapped the image of Oliver. "How did you know him?"

As he spoke, Greyson kept his eyes on the photos. "When you came to the works the other day, I didn't know it were him you were on about. You had no photo and no name. Neither my workforce or me knew anything about any murder. We still don't. Today you show me these. I admit, I do recognise him, but that's as far as it goes. He were looking for work, that's all. We had nowt, so I told him to sling his hook. But he hung around. In the end I had to get shirty just to get rid."

"Why should we believe you?"

"Because it's the truth. He probably took the nuts and bolts while he were in my yard."

Elwyn shook his head. "Why would he do that?" I doubt he'd waste his time. Has there been anyone else hanging around looking for work since then?"

"We get folk calling from time to time. But him," he nodded at the photos, "he were a mad bugger. As well as a job, he kept going on about some report or other. I'd no idea what he was on about, but he didn't want to listen. Kept insisting I had it and that he knew it was fake."

"Did you see him leave your premises?" Elwyn asked.

"Eventually."

"He came back later, climbed over your fence. The film shows him doing it. I'm surprised your alarms weren't triggered. What was your nightwatchman doing while the lad was breaking in?"

The two detectives watched Greyson wrestle with this. "I'll have to ask him. He never reported anything."

Rachel smiled. "We'll ask him ourselves, don't worry."

"Have you two done now?" Greyson said. "I've got a meeting to go to and it's getting late."

"We'll be wanting to speak to your staff, particularly your watchman. I'll be in touch." Rachel said.

Greyson was allowed to leave. Rachel gathered up the photos and put them back in the folder. "What was Oliver doing breaking in, Elwyn? More to the point, what was he looking for? Not a few nuts and bolts, that's for sure. That report Frodsham asked Greyson about, what was that, I wonder?"

"Who knows? Greyson was no help. Whatever is going on, he doesn't want to say."

"There has to be something. Oliver was interested enough to risk being caught when he went over that fence."

"It could be about that piece of land," Elwyn suggested. "It is right next to Greyson's place. It would make sense, if he wanted to extend his business."

"You think we should have asked him?" She shook her head. "I doubt we'd have got anywhere. Greyson wasn't up for telling us anything. But you're right. My gut says that land is important. But we need to make some enquiries first, get our facts straight. Finding out what is planned for the land will do for starters."

"Alice?" Elwyn asked, checking his watch. "Up to it?"

"Yeah, why not? Then a takeaway and home."

"Er, my stuff?"

"Can we do that tomorrow? By the time we've spoken to Alice, we'll be totally knackered."

CHAPTER SEVENTEEN

Rachel pulled up outside Alice Brough's address. "Nice area," Elwyn said.

It was a large detached house, built in the fifties. "I know. That's why I live here too." She glanced at him, smiling. "You do know where we are?"

Elwyn shrugged.

"Our cottage is about half a mile away, that's all."

"Background?" Elwyn asked.

"Her dad is fairly well-heeled. But he works hard for it and is away a lot, leaving her at home alone for long periods of time. Over the last few years that's made Alice more insular than is good for a teenage girl. She has a tendency to become obsessed with things, ideas and people. For a while I was concerned about how attached she was to Megan."

"Are they the same age?"

"Yes, although I think Alice is young for her age. Sometimes she comes across as almost childlike." Rachel pressed the doorbell. "We'll go easy. Alice is emotionally delicate. There has been no mother on the scene since she was very young. Her father tries, but he's too wrapped up in his work."

Alice answered the door. "Mrs King?" She looked puzzled. "Megan isn't here."

Rachel gave her a friendly smile. The girl had her hair tied in the usual plaits, and she was wearing a fake fur onesie. Rachel gave Elwyn a discreet nudge. She didn't want any smart comments. "I know. It's you we'd like to talk to. Can we come in?"

Alice stood aside and gestured towards the living room. "This isn't a social call then?"

"No. We're here to ask you some questions about Oliver Frodsham," Rachel said.

"Ask away. But I won't pretend I'm sorry he's dead," she admitted. "I'm glad. He deserved everything he got, and more. I've heard the rumours, and I hope he suffered."

Rachel was taken aback by her outburst. This wasn't the Alice she knew. "That's harsh. You surprise me."

"You have no idea what he was like." She spoke sharply. "Ask Megan, she knew."

"The lad is dead, Alice. Murdered in the most horrific way," Rachel said gently.

"He deserved it, and more. He played the most awful trick on me. I can never forgive that. He made me the laughing stock of our class at college. I have a hard enough time fitting in as it is without help from morons like him. Most folk saw only one side to Ollie. But it was all a sham. In reality, he was crafty and underhand, and even violent. I tackled him about his methods once. He just said that was how he needed to be to get what he wanted."

"And what was that?"

"His own way."

The hatred was real. Rachel saw the steel in her eyes. A side of Alice that was both shocking and new to her. This Alice was a world away from the mild-mannered, soft-spoken girl who'd often eaten at their house.

"When did you see him last?" Elwyn asked.

"The day he died. You found his body the following morning, so it must have been."

"How was he then?"

"Just as hateful as ever. Kept going on about how he'd taken me in, what a soft touch I was. I gave him money, you know. I'd have done anything for him. I really thought he was my Alfie."

It dawned on Rachel just what a huge deal this was for Alice. Her search for her twin brother, Alfie, had dominated her young life. But was the joke he'd played on her a good enough motive for murder? "Do you have an alibi for the night Oliver was killed?"

"I saw him that afternoon outside uni. I went to a lecture at two. It finished at three thirty, and then I came home."

"Was anyone else here?"

"No. My dad's away, some conference in Amsterdam." She thought for a moment. "Oh, Sarah was here. She lives up the road. Her mother made me some tea and Sarah brought it round. We got talking, opened a bottle of wine, and she didn't leave until gone midnight."

So that was that. According to Butterfield, the lad was already dead by then. Providing her alibi stuck, that ruled Alice out.

"You said you gave him money. How much?"

"Five hundred. He said he needed it to get some new clothes and stuff. I let him stay here too, when my dad was away."

"Didn't you consider telling your dad about Oliver being Alfie?" asked Rachel. "That would have been the obvious way to go."

"My dad refuses to admit that Alfie ever existed." Alice sifted through a pile of papers on a coffee table by the sofa. "Here, look at this, Mrs King. You'll understand this stuff."

She handed Rachel a birth certificate. It was indeed for an Alfie Brough, and the parents had the same names as Alice's. "This is my birth certificate." She handed Rachel another document. "Same day, date, parents — everything in fact."

"Is it genuine?" Elwyn was looking over Rachel's shoulder.

"Yes. The question is, is this a coincidence or not? Another Alfie Brough, born to parents with the same surname as yours, Alice."

"Born and registered on the same date! I've been to see the registrar, checked the register myself. You're as bad as my dad. He said exactly the same thing." Her face twisted in anger. "I'm sick of having to keep saying it. The boy named on that certificate is my twin brother! I remember him, then he disappeared. No one took it seriously at the time, so what chance do I have, all these years later?"

"How can that be true?" Elwyn asked, puzzled. "Children don't just go missing without a big hue and cry. What about your mother? She would have been desperate."

"I don't know what she did. No one will tell me anything."

"Where is your mother, Alice?" Elwyn asked.

"No one will tell me that either. She just disappeared. My father doesn't seem to care. They were always fighting anyway."

"Was there someone else?" Rachel asked.

"No. He hasn't been out with another woman since."

"Do you have any other proof that your brother existed?" Rachel asked her.

"I have this." She passed over a photo. It showed a woman standing with a small child on either side of her, a boy and a girl. She was smiling happily, and so were the children.

"Me, my mother and Alfie in the garden of this house. We would have been about five."

"Which hospital were you born in, Alice?"

"Stockport," Alice said.

"I don't understand how your father can deny this." Rachel handed the photo back. "You have a certificate, a photo . . . why doesn't he just tell you what happened?"

"Because I think he killed them."

CHAPTER EIGHTEEN

It was early evening, dusk just beginning to fall. The man usually stayed out of sight at this time, too many prying eyes. But today was different. Today was the day Luke had agreed to meet him.

He'd done the best he could to disguise himself. Trimmed the newly grown facial hair into a neat beard and moustache and dyed his hair a shade darker. He was tall, and not bad-looking for his age but no oil painting. Studying his reflection in the mirror, he was pleased at what he saw. He'd done the best he could. He looked at his expensive shirt and tie, and his smart suit. With the addition of a wallet full of money, he'd be irresistible.

He took the train into the city, and then it was a short walk from the station to Canal Street. The crisp evening air would clear his head. He wouldn't drink too much either. He needed to keep his wits sharp. His plans were going too well to botch things up by getting pissed.

He'd done his research, found a name and used it cleverly. Soon the police would have the lead they must be frantic for, a lead that would keep them going round in circles for some time to come.

He'd been on a high since the killing. It felt great but exhausting. Luke would be next, following the same pattern but at a different venue. He knew a street where the houses were due for demolition and stood empty. Like the last place, this one too was close to the canal. The land had been bought by the council, and the plans were still being argued over. The perfect place for a little fun.

The outside table that he'd earmarked was empty. He began to feel nervous. This was important, it had to go right. He called to a waiter and ordered a bottle of red and two glasses. The alcohol would calm him down. All he had to do now was wait.

"Excuse me, sir."

The man looked up. He was young, pretty, but with dark hair. Not Luke — pity. Nonetheless, he offered him a drink.

"No thanks." The young man smiled and backed off slightly. "I'm a police officer, name's DC Farrell. Would you mind looking at this photo? And would you tell me if you've seen the young man around here recently?"

Heart in mouth time. But the police couldn't be onto him so soon, surely? The man took a closer look at the copper and could see he was nervous. He was clearly inexperienced, well out of his comfort zone among the gay bars of Canal Street. No need to worry. This was exactly what it looked like — the police were fishing.

"The photo, sir." The policeman thrust it in front of him.

And there he was, his first victim, fresh as a daisy. Standing not two metres from where they were now. "What's he done?" He handed the snap back, forcing a smile.

"He got himself murdered."

"Oh dear. I'm sorry." He sounded sincere. He was good at this. "But I can't help, I'm afraid. I don't know the lad." That was true, he didn't. He'd killed him, not cultivated him as a friend. "Why not ask inside the bar? Someone in there might be able to help."

The man saw the hesitation on the detective's face. "You're nervous, aren't you? Don't be. First time in a gay bar?" He smiled and patted the hand holding the photo. "Don't worry, we don't bite."

"James?" A voice called from behind. "Sorry I'm late."

"Luke!" The man smiled.

The detective and Luke regarded each other for a second or two and exchanged nods, then Luke sat down at the table.

"I'll leave you to it." The detective tore his eyes from the couple, and scuttled off.

"Anxious and twitchy. First time in this neck of the woods, I reckon," the man said, smiling.

"Was he chatting you up?" Luke asked.

"Good heavens no!"

"Damn buses are running late again. There's been an accident. Traffic is backed up all through the northern quarter," Luke said.

He was annoyed, possibly even jealous. That amused the man. He looked at him. Yes, it was all there. The golden hair, the angelic face with big eyes, and the petulant mouth. He had chosen well.

"No matter. You're here now. Nice to meet you." The man poured him a generous glass of wine. "Drink this, and relax. That guy I was talking to was a policeman. Some poor soul got himself murdered near here, and he's making enquiries."

"I read about that in the papers. So young. Such a tragic waste of a life. He was good-looking too."

The man changed the subject quickly. "Have you been here before?" He was genuinely curious. He couldn't recall ever seeing Luke on Canal street.

"Perhaps once or twice, that's all. I don't live local." He took a slug of the wine. "I really do hate being late, I'm sorry. It wasn't deliberate.

"Stop stressing, it's fine. Besides, the detective kept me company."

"Do you come here a lot?" Luke asked.

"I love the place. The atmosphere, the people I meet, there's nowhere like it."

"You're not like your profile photo." Luke gave him a sly smile.

"Now it's me who should apologise. But a bloke has to try. A little help from the software, or I'd get nowhere. It's not all about what we look like though, is it?"

Luke shook his pretty head, his golden curls ruffling in the light breeze. The man closed his eyes for a moment. This boy was perfection.

CHAPTER NINETEEN

Wednesday

"Is there a problem, DCI King?" Harding asked.

The truth was, Rachel didn't know. What to tell him? Right now, she wished that Alice Brough had kept her big mouth shut. But she hadn't, so Rachel had no choice but to take it further.

"DS Pryce and I went to see Alice Brough yesterday evening, making enquiries regarding the Frodsham murder. She told us something unexpected, and I don't think we can ignore it."

Rachel saw the stare. He wasn't happy. Complications were not something Harding countenanced, and this was a biggy. She inhaled, bracing herself. "Alice Brough accused her father, Alexander, of killing her mother and brother. If it is true, sir, it happened almost twelve years ago."

Rachel saw the twitch, high on the cheekbone in his otherwise immobile face. She'd seen it before. He was shaken. He liked order. Things went awry, he didn't cope well. This case, with its many ramifications, was getting to him. Harding was just about keeping it together.

He coughed. "The girl could be fantasising, you know. I've looked at the reports that have come in so far. She's an only child, often left alone. She could have made this up, a ploy to get attention."

"It is a good possibility that she's mistaken, sir. Alice is an odd one. However, she does have compelling evidence that a brother did exist, something her father apparently denies, and always has."

"The mother?"

"Not on the scene. Not since Alice was a child. As far as she recalls, they disappeared at the same time. Not spoken about either. It's like the woman, just like Alice's brother, never existed."

"And neither Ms Brough nor her father has ever reported this?"

"No, sir."

"And you're sure she simply didn't leave and take the child with her? If there is no record of the disappearance then there must have been a plausible explanation. People would have asked at the time where she was. Brough must have told them something. Why's it coming up now?"

"Alice knew Oliver Frodsham from college. They didn't get on. In fact, and Alice makes no bones about it, she hated him. Oliver played a cruel trick on her. He pretended to be her long-lost brother. I think that's what caused her to tell us. And she's friendly with my daughter, Megan, so she trusts me. I did consider that it might be a motive for his murder, but she has provided an alibi. We're checking that now.

"She didn't simply tell you this tale out of spite?"

"I doubt it, sir. Alice has always had a thing about finding her brother, and everyone who knows her is well aware of it."

"Do you know the father?" Harding asked.

"I've met him a couple of times."

"What's your opinion?"

"He seems a straightforward sort of man. He's in his mid-forties, works hard. He could spend more time at home, but the two of them seem to muddle through."

Harding sat in silence, obviously considering what Rachel had told him. She wished he'd hurry up and decide, and then they could get on with it.

"You've spoken to the father about this?" he asked eventually.

Rachel shook her head. "He is away working until the weekend."

"I'll appoint another team to look into it." This was not what Rachel wanted to hear. "DCI Bridges, I think. Give him the information you've gathered, and the background."

"Isn't DCI Bridges on leave, sir? It might be better to allow my team to start the preliminary investigation. It does dovetail with our existing enquiry."

Harding's eyes narrowed. Now she was for it. He didn't take well to criticism.

He pointed to the door. Dismissed. "Not your problem."

Not your problem. That didn't add up to leave it alone, well, not really. Perhaps she would risk it. At least make a few enquiries, get the ball rolling and see where it went. She could check if Alice's mother actually gave birth to twins. After that, a word with the girl's father.

CHAPTER TWENTY

Now they had ruled Alice out, they must look at what else they had. Rachel called over to the information officer, Stella. "Find out everything you can about that piece of land by the canal. Who owns it, what's planned — you know the stuff. And it's urgent. I'll lay odds that it's the land that's at the bottom of that dispute between Oliver and Greyson."

"If Greyson wants it, wouldn't he simply ask the owners?" Elwyn said. "If the land is for sale, given his firm's proximity to it, I would imagine he would have approached him anyway."

"Until we get all the facts, we can't presume anything. Dynamite, Oliver reckoned. The way he was living is bound up in this somehow. He was living rough from choice, not necessity. I'm sure Greyson was lying to us yesterday — my gut told me. He knows a lot more. One way or another, we need to find evidence that forces him to come clean."

"Ma'am, I took a team of uniformed officers and spoke to the workforce at Greyson's. It's as we suspected, no one knows or saw anything."

"Thanks, Amy." She could have predicted that one. Rachel stood in front of the incident board, looking at the photos she'd put up of Greyson and Alice Brough. "She's an interesting one.

We might have ruled her out as a suspect, but I'd still like to clarify what happened during that spat she had with Oliver in the canteen," she told Elwyn. "Weird. I thought I knew that girl, now she's coming across as a complete stranger."

"One of the uniforms spoke to her friend, Sarah. Alice's alibi checks out. Why waste valuable time and resources raking up the fight in the canteen? We know it didn't lead anywhere," Elwyn said.

"It's my gut again. Now I've seen this other side to Alice, it's bothering me, given how close she is to Megan. I just want a rounded picture, that's all. And then there's what she said about her father." She shook her head. "What did you think about that, Elwyn?"

"I'd put it down to an overactive imagination, but it does merit checking out. You've met the family. Do you see the father being a killer?"

Elwyn had a point. But the missing twin was troubling Rachel. What if he really did exist? Prove he existed, find where he and the mother were, and her mind would be at rest.

"Harding thinks the mother left and took Alfie with her. We can't rule that out. But if that's what happened why doesn't Brough tell her?"

"Perhaps he's ashamed, blames himself and wants to forget the event entirely."

Rachel wasn't convinced. The violent streak Alice had exhibited made her nervous. Rachel couldn't get it out of her head that it might be at the bottom of the mystery.

"I got nowhere with Canal Street, ma'am," Jonny said. "I spoke to loads of people, showed the lad's photo around, but nothing."

"Doesn't surprise me. I doubt he was a regular. He was probably just chancing his arm, begging round the tables. For reasons connected to some project of his, he was pretending to be a homeless person."

"We mustn't forget the villain Oliver was allegedly working for," Elwyn said. "Might be an idea to find out who that was."

Rachel nodded. She didn't want to push that particular aspect until she knew more, particularly who this crook actually was. That way she stayed in control. "Jonny, you and Amy go and have a word with Greyson's nightwatchman. I want to know why the alarm didn't go off, and why he said he saw nothing. I think he's lying. Find out why. This time of day, he'll be at home. Get the address and go see him."

"There was a call for you earlier, ma'am," Amy said. "Jason Fox from forensics."

"You should have told me that immediately," Rachel snapped. "We're waiting on them." She went into her office to ring him back. They had two suspects in the frame — well, almost. It would be the forensics that swung it.

Dr Jason Fox was head of the forensic department they worked with. He was a pleasant bloke, her own age and unmarried, although he'd had a fair few relationships. He liked Rachel and made no secret of it. He'd asked her out numerous times, but she'd always refused. Not because she didn't like him, because she did, but just not that way, not with Jed McAteer dominating her thoughts.

"DCI King. Long time no speak. I've missed you."

"Only because you've been sunning yourself abroad somewhere, Jason. What have you got for me?"

"There was Diazepam in his system, so he was definitely drugged. He'd been drinking too."

"Any Rohypnol?" she asked.

"Can't tell. It leaves the system very quickly. Not much chance by the time we got to him, I'm afraid. Something interesting though. There was a wound on his upper arm. It was deep, possibly inflicted with a knife."

"Not part of the attack he was subjected to before he died?"

"I'd say not. The skin on his upper arm wasn't too badly damaged and the wound had started to heal. I'd say it happened a week, perhaps ten days ago."

"Could it be the sort of wound you might get defending yourself?" Rachel asked. She was thinking about the fight with Alice.

"Possibly, we're still doing tests. But you have to understand these are taking time because of the condition of the body."

"He was skinny, obviously didn't look after himself. Perhaps his money was going on the drugs and not food? You still working on the crime scene?"

"We've got our work cut out there. It's going to take a while. Anything interesting and you'll be the first to know. There is something else. It's for you to decide if it's important or not. Those nuts and bolts we found, we did tests on them. No prints, but we did find traces of arsenic."

Rachel was puzzled. "I don't understand. How does that happen?"

"Like I said, it was only a trace. It could have come from the soil. Something for you to think about. You might consider whether that wasteland is contaminated. Check it out. There'll be records, reports somewhere. That could be the reason it has never been developed."

She put the phone down. Perhaps that's what Frodsham wanted to find when he broke into Greyson's. But what did it mean? She checked the time. They needed to know more about Alice's background, but the day was going by. They still had to have another word with the students at the uni, see who witnessed the barney between her and Oliver. Rachel wanted to know how many times, if any, Alice had lost it in the past.

Back in the incident room, she had a word with Stella.

"Investigations into that piece of land have just gone up a notch. Get onto the land registry. Find out who owns it. When that's done, we want names of all parties who have shown an interest in buying it. And any reports of soil tests."

CHAPTER TWENTY-ONE

"I reckon this is a waste of time," said Amy. She and Jonny pulled up outside the house in Failsworth where Douglas Croft, the nightwatchman at Greyson's, lived. "The alarm will have failed or perhaps Frodsham tampered with it beforehand."

"The boss says we speak to him, so that's what we do," Jonny said. He wasn't about to be led into a slag-off-the-boss session.

"And she knows best! Listen to yourself! She does get it wrong, you know. She made a right cock-up of the Hindle case last year."

"I wasn't here last year," said Jonny. "Everything I've seen so far tells me DCI King is okay. She knows what's she's doing."

"Right little boss's pet you're turning into," Amy scoffed. "She'll have you running after her with cups of tea next."

"From what I've seen, that's Pryce's job," he said, grinning. "I reckon he's got the hots for her. Cut out the work crap and they wouldn't make a bad couple."

"Don't make me laugh. Pryce wouldn't waste his time."

"Why so down on her?" Jonny asked.

"She doesn't like me, made that plain from the off." Amy flicked her hair behind her ears. "I was hoping to go for DS soon. What are my chances with her as my boss? Nil, I'd say."

"I think you've got her all wrong. She takes the job seriously, that's all. It's not a question of liking or disliking a particular colleague."

"Wish I could get something on her," Amy said. "I'd love to see ma'am squirm, get the rough end for a change. I get the impression Harding would like that too. The big boss isn't keen on her either."

Jonny had heard enough. "Let's find this bloke and get it over with."

They got out of the car and went up to the front door. "Bedroom curtains are shut tight. I reckon he's in bed." Jonny knocked loudly.

"Works nights, who can blame him? Hey up, he's just peeped out at us." Amy smiled.

More banging, and a few raps on the front window finally brought a response. A middle-aged man wearing a dressing gown opened the door.

"What d'you want? I'm not buying anything."

"Police." Amy flashed her badge. "We'd like to ask you a few questions."

He hesitated, looked them up and down. "Alright, come in, but I don't have long." He showed them into the sitting room.

Jonny showed him the photo of Oliver Frodsham. "Do you remember the day this man came to your work premises?"

"No. Should I?"

"He broke in at night," Amy said. "You're the security person. So, yes, you should remember."

"You must be mistaken."

Amy shook her head. "We know he was there. We have him on CCTV, talking to Mr Greyson. Later that same night he climbed in over your fence."

Douglas Croft suddenly turned and went into the kitchen. "Don't know nowt, me," he called back. "You'd be best asking Greyson."

"We did, and he pointed us in your direction," Amy said.

Croft's body language told them all they needed to know. He clearly knew exactly what they were getting at and didn't have an answer. They followed him into the kitchen.

"Why didn't the alarm go off, Mr Croft?" Jonny asked.

He grunted. "Must have been faulty."

"Did you see him?"

Croft's hands were shaking. He had his back to them, aimlessly opening cupboard doors. "I've got nowt to say. I don't know why I didn't see him, but I didn't."

"Were you asleep perhaps?" Jonny asked.

"No. Sacking offence, that is."

"Then I don't understand. Greyson speaks highly of you and the security system he has installed. I'll ask you again, what happened?" Jonny said. He moved a little closer to Croft.

Croft went back into the sitting room and poured himself a tot of brandy from a bottle on the sideboard, then threw himself into an armchair. He had gone grey in the face and looked like he was about to collapse. "Got me in a right state this has. You're harassing me. I said I can't help you."

"We're not harassing you, Mr Croft. It's a simple question," Amy said. "Were you helping Frodsham? Do you know what he hoped to find at Greyson's?"

"I've no idea," he muttered.

"Speak up, Mr Croft," Jonny urged. "Just tell us what you know and we'll leave you in peace."

Croft shook his head. "I knew it wouldn't work. I said so at the time."

"What wouldn't work, Mr Croft?" Jonny asked.

"I should have remembered to doctor that film, taken out the bit with the lad in it. If I had, you'd never have been the wiser."

Amy looked at Jonny. "Are you admitting that you helped Oliver Frodsham that night?"

"That's not what I said."

"It amounts to the same thing," Amy said.

He poured himself more brandy. "I can't take pressure. I'm bad with my nerves as it is." He paused. "He said he'd pay me, but that never happened. Said that if he got what was needed, I'd get more. All I had to do was turn off the alarm for a little while. Turn a blind eye and let the lad get on with it."

"What did Frodsham do?"

"He got into Greyson's office. Said he was after some documents. I've no idea what they were and that's the truth."

"How much money were you promised?" Amy asked.

"A grand, with another to come later."

"How did Frodsham hope to manage that?" Amy said. "He was a student."

"No idea, and I didn't ask."

Amy watched him closely. He was keeping something back, couldn't look them in the eye. "Was Frodsham working for someone else? A rival of Greyson's perhaps?"

"How would I know?"

"What are you afraid of exactly?" Jonny asked.

"All these questions, you're giving me a headache."

"He was, wasn't he?" Amy said. "And it was that someone else who told you to turn a blind eye and was going to pay you."

That got a reaction alright. For a moment Amy thought he was going to fly at her.

"Okay, the lad didn't hire or pay me. But it wasn't no rival. It were some villain. The nasty bugger came here to this house, and threatened me. He and Greyson are fighting over that land. Both of them are playing dirty, but as usual it's the little people who get caught in the crossfire."

The two detectives looked at each other. They hadn't expected this.

"Does he have a name, this villain?" Jonny asked.

"I talk and my life won't be worth living. I live on my own. I wouldn't last the week."

Amy took Jonny to the hallway for a moment. "We could offer him protection. What d'you think?"

"We'd have to clear it with DCI King."

Back in the sitting room, Amy regarded Croft closely. "That is some allegation you've made."

"Do you think I don't know that? Scared witless, I've been."

"Tell us who this villain is and we'll put you in a place of safety. You can trust us." She meant it. A quick word with the boss and they could have the man in a safe house within the hour.

Croft thought about this, turning his bleary gaze from one to the other. He sighed. "Couldn't carry on like this anyway. I'll get taken out one day when I least expect it. That way I never talk and they stay safe."

"His name, Mr Croft," Amy urged.

"Liam Beatty."

Jonny nudged her arm. "Who's Beatty?"

"Not someone you mess with," she whispered. "One of the real bad guys." She turned to Croft. "You're far safer trusting us. You know who Beatty works for?"

Croft was still shaking. "Course I do. The whole of Manchester knows that."

Jonny nudged her again. "I've no idea who you're talking about."

"He's Jed McAteer's right hand man."

Jonny was no wiser. "And he is?"

"Something of a crime baron around these parts."

CHAPTER TWENTY-TWO

"Is something up?" Elwyn said. "You're very quiet today."

"It's the case. Something needs to break." It was a lie. What was bothering Rachel was Jed. She pulled into a parking space at the side of the college and turned off the engine. "Forensics are still working on the crime scene. This whole thing, the way Frodsham died, it smacks of a psycho. As for Frodsham's body, the only new thing we have to go on is the knife wound. That was down to Alice, and we know she didn't kill him. Whoever did, took their time, possibly even planned it. We're missing something, Elwyn."

Rachel was about to say more when her mobile rang.

"Well, well. Aren't you the tricky one to get hold of?"

Rachel's heart began to race. How to deal with this? Not with Elwyn next to her, that was for sure. "Give me a minute alone, could you?" She knew Elwyn would ask questions but what choice did she have?

Once her DS was out of the car, she cleared her throat. Her mouth was so dry that she could barely speak. "This isn't on, Jed. No contact, remember?"

"It's not working for me, babe. What about you? Don't you miss our times together?" Jed said.

"What I miss isn't the issue. We have an agreement. This is stupid. I can't talk to you. You have to leave me alone." Rachel ended the call. She was wound up enough without Jed McAteer ringing her every five minutes.

"You okay?" Elwyn asked. "You're as white as a sheet. Bad news?"

"The worst." She said nothing further.

The two of them walked to reception in silence. Rachel knew Elwyn was holding back, keeping his questions under control. She couldn't do this, she had to offer some explanation. "It's nothing really, just something with the girls." The words sounded stilted, false. Elwyn was no fool, he'd know she was lying. "Meggy's got a boyfriend, with all the problems that go along with it."

"New phase then. You'll have to learn new skills — how to cope with strange young men about the house, for starters."

"And the rest." She laughed unconvincingly.

Rachel saw the look. He knew she was lying to him. He wouldn't let it drop, he never did.

They were expected. Mrs Gaskell had organised a room for them on the ground floor. "I've ordered coffee," she said. "I don't know how I can help, but I'll tell you what I can."

Moments later they heard a knock at the door, Hayley Burton with a tray of coffee. She saw Rachel and smirked. Word had got out. Alice was in bother and no one had any sympathy.

As soon as Hayley left, Rachel turned to Mrs Gaskell. "Tell us about the skirmish between Alice and Oliver Frodsham."

"It all happened so fast. A dozen or so students were queuing for lunch when suddenly Alice lunged at the boy. Called him all sorts of names. Her language was atrocious. He gave as good as he got, though. He called her something I didn't hear, but one of the girls said he'd told her she was a stupid bitch who deserved to be conned. That seemed to set her off. She went berserk, snatched a knife from the cutlery dispenser and flew at him."

"Did she stab him?" Rachel asked.

"Oliver put his arms up to defend himself and suffered a flesh wound to one of them. There was a lot of blood, so to be on the safe side, I took him across the road to the hospital. The wound needed a couple of stitches."

"Was the assault reported?" Rachel asked.

"Oliver said he'd do that. One of the girls said she'd go with him."

Rachel had checked. No report had been made.

"What was their relationship like in general?"

"Non-existent. Oliver only became interested in Alice in the last couple of months. He hung around with some of her friends." Mrs Gaskell smiled at Rachel. "With some of your Megan's friends, actually. Alice was one of the group. Megan took her under her wing. I think he learnt that Alice had money, so he saw his chance and duped her. Everyone knows about Alice's obsession with her twin brother. She spends hours in the library doing research into her family and her parents' background."

"That was very helpful." Rachel could do with that research herself. Even though she knew Alice hadn't killed Oliver, there was something about the girl that bugged her.

"Has Alice ever lost her temper in that way before?" Rachel asked.

"Not that I'm aware of. Normally she's a gentle sort of girl. It's just this brother thing. It seems to rile her."

Rachel and Elwyn went back to the car. "What now?" Elwyn asked, shaking his head. "I'm stumped. I hope the other two are getting better results than we are."

"We're not doing badly. We've ruled out Alice, so now we need to look closer at that land — who wants it and why. Alice took us off track for a while. We were looking in the wrong place, now we have to concentrate on the land issue."

CHAPTER TWENTY-THREE

"Want to talk now?" Elwyn asked, glancing at her.

They were on their way back to the station, Elwyn driving. He knew something was wrong. It was the long face that did it, but Rachel couldn't help that. Jed was a problem with no solution.

"Something's up. I know you. You've hardly said a word since you got that call earlier. And don't fob me off with chat about boyfriends, just tell me the truth. Perhaps I can help."

Rachel heaved a sigh. She could certainly do with someone's help right now, even just a friendly discussion about what to do regarding Jed McAteer. But there was no way she could put that burden on Elwyn. "If I could tell you, I would. But trust me, this is one problem you do not want to share."

"Not down to Megan then? I knew I was right. Try me. Whatever it is, I won't say a word to anyone."

Rachel patted his arm, smiling. "Forget it. I'm being a stupid cow, that's all."

If she confided in him, how would Elwyn react? Jed was a villain. Elwyn wouldn't approve, that was for sure. But would he take any action? If she told him, and Jed was involved in this case or any in the future, he would be in an impossible situation. She couldn't do that to him.

"Let it drop for now. I can't tell you anything, so you're wasting your time."

"Won't tell me anything, you mean. And that makes me edgy." His face pulled into a frown. "But it's big, I can tell. You've not been in a mood like this since your parents."

They drove the rest of the way in silence. He wasn't happy about her refusal to tell him, Rachel knew. He'd be thinking she didn't trust him. Well, there was nothing she could do.

When they arrived back at the station, Rachel called a short meet. She wanted to know what they'd all gleaned this morning. Hopefully, Jonny and Amy had done better than they had.

"The fight in the college canteen took place as described. It was a vicious attack but we've ruled Alice out. She is no longer a person of interest in this case." Rachel hesitated. "And for what it's worth, I think we're looking for a man. The Alice issue has sent us off course. We need to redouble our efforts."

"We've got some juicy info." Amy grinned.

The DC was on pins, fidgeting with her notes and checking her phone. Rachel had rarely seen her so excited. This should be good.

"The nightwatchman, Croft, was very forthcoming — eventually, that is. It turns out that he was paid to turn a blind eye while Frodsham broke in. Croft was promised a backhander to ensure that Frodsham got some documents from Greyson's office."

"Do we know what documents?"

Amy shook her head.

"Paid by who?" Rachel asked.

"This is the juicy bit." Amy paused for effect. "Liam Beatty." Amy sat back with a self-satisfied look on her face.

As well as the team, a number of uniformed officers were also present. There was a buzz as the name echoed around the room. Most of them knew Beatty.

Rachel knew him too, only too well. Liam Beatty was in Jed's pocket, had been for years. He was the man Jed got to do his dirty work. Her instincts had been right. Jed's recent attempts to contact her was down to the case.

"Do we bring him in?" Amy asked.

But in her panic, Rachel hardly heard her. Her head was whirling, her stomach churning. Liam Beatty would never mention Jed. It was more than his life was worth. But the officers she worked with weren't stupid. They knew who was pulling the strings. Rachel had no idea what Beatty knew about her and Jed. Probably nothing, but she couldn't take the risk. If he'd ever heard the merest whisper, he would use it in any interview by pressurising her. If it meant his freedom, he wouldn't hesitate to drop her in it.

"Ma'am?" Amy sounded impatient. "Beatty. Do we bring him in?"

The answer to that had to be a yes. Anything else would invite questions she couldn't answer. But she daren't interview him herself. There was no way she'd be able to hold it together.

"Elwyn, you and Amy bring him in. Interview him, and see what he has to say for himself."

Rachel caught the look on Elwyn's face. He was puzzled, no doubt burning with curiosity as to why she'd delegated, especially to Amy.

"We'll get right on it." He nodded. "Can I have a quick word first?"

Here it came. They marched into her office and he closed the door.

"What's going on?" he asked. "Why pass over the interview with Beatty? He is now a prime suspect. It should be you."

"I can't! And that's all I have to say on the matter. You and Amy will be fine. I've got stuff to do."

She hated lying to Elwyn. And he was right. It should be her. But how could she? One wrong word from Beatty and it would be the end of her job. Jed might hold back but Beatty wouldn't hesitate to drop her in it.

"Is it the girls? Is something wrong?" Elwyn looked concerned.

A lifeline.

"Yes," she lied. "It's Mia. She's been feeling ill all day. Dizzy spells. She's probably not eaten right. I need to check her out. Alan is seeing a client tonight, he can't get out of it, and Megan will panic."

"You should have said. Of course, you go. We'll bring Beatty in, see what he has to say for himself. I'll ring you later, tell you what went on."

"Thanks. I'll make tracks now, if it's all the same. I need to make sure Mia is okay and get her to bed."

Rachel felt terrible deceiving Elwyn, but she had to tell him something. It was a narrow escape, but for how long? If Jed McAteer had anything to do with Frodsham's death she would have to bring him in too. She'd have no choice. And that didn't bear thinking about.

CHAPTER TWENTY-FOUR

Rachel was torn. What to do? She'd done some food shopping in an effort to calm down, and now she was sitting in the supermarket car park, running the day's events through her head. She should ring Jed, blast him for putting her through this. But she daren't. If he was involved with the case in any way, it could jeopardise everything when it went to the courts.

There was nothing for it but to go home. Elwyn would expect her to be there when he rang with an update. She hoped to God Beatty didn't drop her in it. She was about to leave when her mobile rang. She was so edgy, Rachel nearly jumped out of her skin.

It was Jed McAteer.

"We need to talk," he said.

"No."

"Why Liam? What've you dragged him in for? I need him with me."

Rachel bet he did. Jed was no lightweight but he didn't like to get his hands dirty. The team had acted quickly. It had only been an hour.

"Hard luck, Jed. He's being interviewed about a serious offence."

"What offence? That's rubbish. Liam's done nothing wrong. Anyway, he's got a top-notch lawyer with him. He'll be out in no time."

"I can't talk to you, Jed. Until the case is sorted, you need to leave me alone."

"No can do, babe. You will talk to me. I'm not interested in the case anyway. I want to discuss Mia."

Rachel's heart hammered in her chest. *Please, this can't be happening now.* What had he found out, and where from? There was no way she could discuss Mia with him. "She has nothing to do with you." Rachel closed her eyes and muttered a little prayer. *He couldn't know. Please God, don't let him know.* If he found out, it would change their lives forever.

"You should have told me. You owed me that much at least. All these years have gone by, years when I should have been part of her life."

He knew!

Rachel tried to think but her mind was racing. What to tell him? Whatever it was, it had to be good. She had to sound convincing. "I've no idea what you're talking about. I'm hanging up. Don't ring me again. You'll be wasting your time if you do because I won't speak to you."

"Have it your way, Rachel. But you'll soon change your mind, I promise you."

Rachel was furious. She started the car, stuck it in gear and roared out of the carpark. She needed to go home, have a drink and calm down. No one else in the world had the power to upset her like Jed did.

* * *

It was dark now, but the cottage was lit up like a beacon. Inside, she heard music blaring, and laughing voices. Not now, please. She really didn't need the drama. The front door was unlocked. In the hallway, a drunk teenage boy was standing propped up against the wall about to throw up. Rachel grabbed him by the bottom of his T-shirt and flung him outside. What the hell was going on? And where was Alan?

"Megan?" She heard giggles, and then her eldest appeared from the kitchen, looking sheepish.

"A few mates, that's all. Honest." The girl held aloft a vodka bottle.

Megan was obviously drunk too. "Get rid of them now, and clear this bloody mess up! You're a disgrace!"

"Me?" Megan replied in mock outrage. "That's rich, coming from you. Do you know how much you've upset Alice? She's been weeping her face off all day. What were you doing anyway, coming the heavy-handed cop with my bestie?"

"I wasn't heavy-handed and God forbid that *she's* your bestie. The girl's a nutjob."

She'd had enough. A group of kids were swigging cans of lager in the kitchen, throwing the empties out into the garden. The noise they were making was off the scale.

"You've no idea, have you? Alice isn't like you think, Mum. She's mixed up but she's no 'nutjob,' as you put it. Ollie tricked her. Conned her out of money. She'd every right to be angry."

"She flew at him with a knife," Rachel said. "Cut his arm, it left a scar. What do you call that?"

Rachel didn't wait for Megan to reply. She suddenly realised she hadn't seen Mia. "Where's your sister?"

"Ella's, I think. There's a note on the table."

"No there isn't."

"Soz, Ma, someone must have moved it. Give her a ring."

Rachel pulled her phone from her pocket. It was late. Mia should be here, or next door with her dad.

"What's going on? Why all the noise?" Alan appeared in the kitchen doorway. "I've just seen a client off and I don't think he was particularly impressed."

"Letting off steam." Megan giggled and made a swift exit.

"Have you seen Mia?" Rachel demanded. Alan shook his head. Rachel's anxiety was mounting. Why wasn't she at home?

"Ah, I remember," he said. "Something about homework and going to her mate's house straight after school."

Mia's phone was turned off. That was not supposed to happen. Rachel used it to track where Mia was. Now she was jittery. She rang Ella's mum. Beth Palmer confirmed that Mia had been to their house but that she'd had a call from her uncle, who'd picked up both the girls. "He's taken them bowling and for a burger. He missed her birthday apparently and wanted to make up. He's a nice man, Alan's brother. He promised to have them back by ten. Mia was happy enough. They chatted away for ages on the phone."

Rachel was stunned. This was nonsense. What uncle? Alan didn't have a brother, so what was going on? "Where exactly did they go, Beth?"

"The bowling alley by the park in Macclesfield."

"Mia told me nothing about this. You should've let me know."

"I'm sorry, I didn't realise it was such a big deal. Mia seemed excited, so was Ella. I presumed she'd cleared it with you, otherwise I would have done something. At the very least, I'd have rung you first."

"I wish you had. And it is a big deal. Mia's thirteen years old. She isn't allowed to just go off with anyone who rings her."

Beth Palmer sounded worried. "But it was her uncle. She said she'd been out with him before. They're not in any sort of trouble or danger, are they?"

Rachel would have to calm down. She could barely believe what was happening, but it would do no good to frighten Beth. "It's alright. It's just me fussing. What with Mia's condition, you know how it is. I have no idea if she's even taken her meds this evening. When did they leave your house?"

"A couple of hours ago."

"Alan has two brothers," Rachel lied. "Which one was it?"

"Mia said it was her Uncle Jed."

CHAPTER TWENTY-FIVE

The voice came from behind him. "Working late, Paul? I suppose that's one of the drawbacks of running your own business."

Paul Greyson was locking the main yard gates. He and Mrs Andrews, his secretary, had finished for the day. He spun round. "You! You got what you wanted the last time, so why are you here? Just leave me alone."

"I have no idea what you mean. I don't like your tone much either."

"You can get off," Greyson said to Mrs Andrews. "I'll deal with this."

The man held up his hand. "No, you can wait here."

"This has nothing to do with her," Greyson blustered. "Let her go."

"You stress too much, Paul. You should think about your blood pressure. I don't mean you any harm."

"No harm? That's a lie. You paid that robbing little git to break in and steal from my office. You didn't have to do that. What's wrong with coming to see me, if you needed money, we could have discussed it properly?"

"I prefer to do things my way. Anyway, it wasn't just money I was after." He leaned forward and smiled. "What I really want is that report. The one that states that land out there has been cleaned up."

"What report? You're talking rubbish. That land is contaminated, no one dare touch it. He took cash out of my desk drawer, that's all, and he scared my watchman half to death. Terrified he is. On medication now. Get lost before I call the police."

"Give me the report and I'll leave you in peace."

"I haven't a clue what you're talking about." He turned to Mrs Andrews. "Do you hear him? The man's mad."

"Some people won't be pleased if I go back empty-handed. I'd change your attitude if I were you, Paul."

"Threats now." Greyson turned to face the man. "What will you do? Tell whoever is paying you how uncooperative I am? Send 'em my way, I'll tell them what a liar you are." Greyson turned to Mrs Andrews. "This one is rambling. There is no report, he's making it up. And even if there was, what would I be doing with it?"

"The people I work for won't like it. They like things to run smooth."

"I was right, you're working for some villain. Who? McAteer? Come on, at least tell me that much."

"Can't do that. He wouldn't like it," the man said.

Pushing Mrs Andrews behind him, Greyson moved closer to the man. "I don't know what your game is, but you know as well as I do that there is no report. That land is just as contaminated now as it always was. Go on, bugger off, or I'll get the law. There's one I've got real interested. All I have to do is say the word, and she'll be round here like a shot."

"Really? You surprise me. Why would the police take an interest in you, Paul?"

"Because of what you did."

"Not me. That was down to the lad. That robbing little git, as you called him, didn't deliver. Offer him a higher price, did you?"

Greyson regarded the man closely. He was trying to decide whether he was lying or not. "What's all this about?

There is no report, you must know that." Greyson was genuinely puzzled.

The man looked at Mrs Andrews. Good, his plan was working, she was taking in every word. "Bad move. We don't want to antagonise the boss and his business partner, do we?"

"Who are these people you're working for?"

"Can't say, Paul. That would really annoy them."

"You always were a mad bugger. Go on, get off before I make that call."

"That's a pity, Paul. I was hoping we could strike a deal. Prevent a lot of unnecessary aggravation. You see, if I go away empty-handed tonight, you're in big trouble."

The man broke into a grin. He was tall, expensively dressed, the type who could charm your socks off, but underneath he was an animal. Suddenly, Greyson was terrified.

"Money, you said. I think there's a couple of grand in the safe. Mrs Andrews can go and get it." He nodded at her.

But the man took hold of her arm. "I'll tell you when."

"I don't understand what all the fuss is about," Greyson blustered. "It's just a piece of derelict land."

"Not quite, Paul, and we both know it. That land is valuable, and the report you're sitting on makes it doubly so. City centre location and all that. A certain someone has sat on it for a long time and now he wants a return on his investment. The businessman who owns the land faked that report and used it to tempt a buyer. He's a developer like the owner. City centre location means top money for anything that gets built." The man nodded. "The truth about what's out there is hush-hush. No one must find out."

"That's a load of bull! There's no buyer and no report. Now do one!"

"This little patch you're sitting on is valuable too. Go along with the plan, and there'll be sure to be a hefty backhander in it for you."

Greyson wasn't budging. "I know nothing about any of that."

The man tilted his head slightly, and stared back. "I can't believe you haven't been offered a deal too." He paused. "It could still work that way. Give me that report and you'll come out of this quids in." The man gave Mrs Andrews the keys. "Get me that money from the safe. No phone calls, mind, or he suffers."

They watched her disappear into the darkness of the yard. Greyson longed to follow her. There was safety behind that tall steel fence. He turned and faced the man again.

"What's this really about? You know as well as I do there is no report and no scam about that land either."

"Just playing a little game, Paul. Shame you didn't join in. Your secretary there took in every word. She has an important part to play. When the police question her, she'll say things I want them to hear. It's all part of the bigger plan. Best if you go with the flow."

"Whatever this is about, it has nowt to do with me."

The man walked towards him, hands balled into fists. "You look twitchy, Paul. Not thinking of doing anything stupid, are you? And where's that woman got to?"

"She'll be back. You can trust her."

"Can I though? She doesn't know it, but that woman is vital to my plans. You see she will send the police into a tailspin searching for the wrong people." The man was almost on top of him. Greyson backed off. "Look, I'm not strong. I don't do self-defence or anything like that. If I knew what you were on about and if I had the damned report, I'd give it to you. But I don't."

"Sorry, Paul, I don't have time to explain. But no need to stress about the report anymore. I know it doesn't exist." He pulled a face. "Oops, shouldn't have said that. Now you're a liability."

"I won't say anything, if that's what you're worried about. You can trust me. Take the money and get out of here."

"Sorry, far too risky. I don't want to do this, honestly. But I have no choice."

The man pulled a handgun from his overcoat pocket.

"Don't do this. Please, go now!" Greyson shouted. "I won't say anything to the police. You can trust me."

The man smiled, a terrifying smile. "I learned a long time ago that you can't trust anybody."

A shot rang out, and Greyson hit the ground.

CHAPTER TWENTY-SIX

Rachel's heart was in her mouth. *Uncle Jed*? Jed was no uncle, not to Mia or anyone else. Nonetheless, it had better be him, the alternative was too horrendous to contemplate. She sat in her car outside the house and scrolled through the contacts on her mobile until she found him.

"Jed!" she screamed. "Is she with you!"

He took his time to reply — tosser!

"Who, babe? Who've you lost?"

Rachel was in no mood for games. He knew very well who she meant. "Mia! Did you take her? Simple question. Now give me an answer."

"Calm down. Both Mia and her mate are quite safe. I was about to drop them off at yours when you rang."

"And I was about to mobilise the troops, report her missing. You bloody idiot! Don't you dare do anything like that again. What did you hope to gain?"

"A little time with my daughter."

The noise of the debacle going on inside her house faded into the background. The only noise Rachel could hear now was the beat of her heart. *He did know*. She closed her eyes. How had that happened? How had he even realised?

"I would never be so stupid. If that's what you think, you're deluded. She's Alan's, not yours."

"DNA doesn't lie, as well you know. Mia is the product of that little interlude we had, fourteen years ago. Remember? That weekend on the Welsh coast. We stayed in that lovely hotel overlooking Cardigan Bay."

She remembered. It had been an idyllic weekend. The weather had been perfect and Jed had been at his most charming. Her defences were down. They'd spent most of their time making love.

"You can't have done a test. I haven't given permission."

"You will. In the meantime, I have eyes in my head. She looks like me."

"In your fantasy! You're grasping at straws. Where are you now?"

"The bowling alley in Macclesfield. Do you know it?"

"Yes. I'm on my way. Don't move until I get there."

Rachel cast a backward glance at the mayhem going on at the cottage. Alan would have to deal with that one. She pulled out and headed towards the main road that would take her into Macclesfield.

What the hell had happened? Mia knew the rules. If Rachel was working, on school nights it was her dad's or Ella's for homework until seven at the latest. Going out was reserved for weekends only. There were no exceptions, unless she was accompanied by a parent.

Her mind was in turmoil. How had Jed got it into his head that Mia was his? He must have seen her recently, perhaps he'd seen them together. He was right on one score. She did look like him, worryingly so. It was most noticeable in her eyes. Jed had lovely eyes, dark and moody. Mia's were the same.

Rachel had suspected she was Jed's for years. She'd spotted the likeness before the child had reached the age of three. There was no way she could live with the uncertainty. It was wrong, and she should have got Alan's permission, but she'd had a DNA test done, Mia and Alan. The result had proved conclusively that Alan wasn't Mia's father. That left only Jed McAteer in the running.

But Rachel had never told Jed, so how did he know? How long had they known each other? At least he'd passed himself off as her uncle and hadn't told her the truth. At all costs, that must never happen.

She wondered just how well they knew each other, Jed and Mia. What did Mia think of him? She'd probably think he was great. He was good-looking and could be utterly charming. He had that way of talking to you as if you were the most important person in the world. He had money too, and wouldn't hesitate to spend it. Mia was young and impressionable. She'd be captivated. Jed McAteer was a world away from Alan King, her supposed father, who'd brought her up.

Rachel pulled into the bowling-alley car park and spotted his black Merc straight away. He was in the driver's seat and the two girls were sitting together in the back, chatting animatedly. She pulled up alongside and wound down her window.

"Get in here, the pair of you," she barked. "And you," she said to Jed, "don't you dare do anything like this again."

Jed appeared amused. "Calm down. There's no need to lose it. The girls have had a great time. Me too."

Mia leaned forward and kissed his cheek. Rachel's heart sank even further. Mia was only thirteen, enjoying herself and obviously impressed. Tell her the truth about this man, what a villain he was, it wouldn't touch the sides. What was his game? Was his affection for real or was it merely a ploy to get to her?

Rachel waited until both girls were in her car and then got out and bent down to his window. "There'll be no more of this. You'll leave her alone," she hissed.

"No. I'll see her again, babe. She likes me. Get used to the idea. Tell the other bloke too. The one passing himself off as her dad. I want a relationship with my daughter. I have rights and you can't stop me."

Other bloke! Jesus. Alan King was an innocent party. *He* was Mia's father. He'd raised her. What was biology after all?

Jed smiled. "I'll phone you. And I've told those two that I'll take them to the cinema this weekend."

"Why tell Mia and her friend that you're her uncle?"

"You'd rather I told her the truth?" He shook his head. "I'm not stupid. I'm leaving that one to you. Mia is young, I'm new in her life." He smiled, and those eyes of his twinkled. "We don't want folk gossiping, do we? You want them to see me with your daughter and think I'm your latest lover? Eh? Better they think I'm an uncle. For now, anyway."

Rachel shook her head. "We're leaving. If you contact her again, I'll have you arrested." It was all she could think of, sheer desperation, and Jed knew it. He simply grinned and waved at the girls.

She and the girls set off for home. Rachel drove in silence.

"I like him," Mia said. "He's fun."

"You don't know him. That man is trouble. As for seeing him, that's another matter. You do nothing until I say so, agreed?"

"He's taking us to see that new film next weekend."

"He isn't, Mia. I mean it. You really want to go, I'll see what I can do. But you leave Jed McAteer out of it."

CHAPTER TWENTY-SEVEN

Thursday

After the day she'd had, and worried by thoughts of what to do about Jed, Rachel tossed and turned for most of the night. She finally gave up early the next morning and was just making coffee when her mobile sounded.

"We've got another body," Elwyn said.

"Please tell me it's not like the last one." The horrific image of Oliver's body spread out on the canal bank came into her head.

"No. Gunshot wound. It's Paul Greyson, shot through the chest. Sometime last night, Butterfield reckons. This one really does look like an execution."

So they were back on that one. "Where?"

"Just outside his yard. And his place has been done over. Whoever is responsible was looking for something. But we do have a witness, his secretary, Mrs Andrews. We had her at the station, but she was in shock. Wasn't making any sense, so we took her home. We'll talk to her later."

"Did she witness the killing?"

"No. She was inside the building, locked in all night. She's in a right state."

It was approaching seven, and the traffic would be building. "I'll be there ASAP. But you know how it is."

Rachel showered and dressed. In the kitchen, Megan was sitting at the table, groaning.

"Serves you right. Drinking's no good for you."

"Save the lecture, Mum. It's only a hangover. I'll live. Honestly, no one's allowed to have any fun around here. Poor Mia. Dragged home in front of her friend. It was embarrassing. She's thirteen, you know. She's not stupid."

"Don't start, Megan. You know nothing about it."

"I know you can't lay down the law to us. We're not kids. Dad was keeping an eye. He was quite happy for my friends to come round."

"What about the booze and the mess? And did he know about Mia?"

"She was at Ella's. Nothing to do with me, that one."

"You are sisters, you look out for each other. You know how she gets."

"Who is that bloke anyway? Mia said he's our uncle, but you've never mentioned him."

"Not now, I'm late for work."

"Bloody work, that's all you do. Can't you put us first for once?"

Rachel had heard enough. "Button it, Megan. I'm in no mood. Clean up the kitchen before you leave, and give Mia her breakfast."

"The mess will have to wait and she'll have to go to Dad's. I've got an early start too. You're not the only one with a life, you know."

Bloody kids! The older they got, the trickier it all became. Megan wouldn't be fobbed off for much longer. Jed was a problem she couldn't explain, but she'd have to find a way.

It took nearly an hour for Rachel to reach Greyson's. A small tent covered the body.

"Looks like a single bullet," Butterfield said. "Close range. Straight into the heart. Death would have been instant." He straightened up and pointed to the tarmac. "That is puzzling. He would not have lived long enough."

The word 'Mac' was written in blood on the concrete.

"His killer?" Jonny asked. "Anyone know who 'Mac' is?"

What could she say? Rachel knew very well what the word meant. It was the nickname Jed's cronies used for him. "We don't know who wrote it. Most likely the killer trying to point the finger elsewhere." Rachel turned to Butterfield.

"What does 'Mac' mean?" Jonny queried again.

Rachel explained briefly. She wasn't comfortable discussing Jed. At least he couldn't have done it. At the time when Greyson was murdered, he was bowling with the girls in Macclesfield. She daren't tell the others this. But Jed had friends, Beatty in particular, and he was a killer.

The huge metal gates were swinging back and forth in the wind and banging. "They must have used the keys. The lock isn't broken."

"Took them off him probably. According to the secretary, he was locking up when the killer pounced," Elwyn said.

"Was it a robbery? Has Mrs Andrews said anything?"

"Not a lot. She said a man was waiting for them in the dark. He approached and wanted some documents off Greyson."

"Not robbery then." Rachel frowned. "Does she know what documents the killer was referring to?"

"No. That was about it. But she does have more to say, she just needs some time."

"Documents? Could they be to do with that land out there?" She nodded at the open stretch in front of them. "Near to where Oliver Frodsham was found. What d'you think?"

"Connected?" Elwyn said.

"Do we know if anything was taken?" Rachel asked.

"Safe is open. Mrs Andrews, that's the secretary, reckons there's usually about two grand in it."

"Anything else?"

"Not that she's aware of. But she'll have a look through the paperwork later and let us know."

Forensics were busy at work. Jason Fox spotted her and waved. "We've got plenty of prints!" he shouted across. "Should have some names for you later today."

Rachel sighed. Frodsham, Greyson, the problem of Alice Brough's missing twin and mother . . . they had a full plate.

"Let's go to the station and get some breakfast," she said. "After that, we'll see if Mrs Andrews is ready to talk. We're doing no good here."

CHAPTER TWENTY-EIGHT

"You're very quiet." Elwyn said.

"Can't eat and talk." Rachel pushed a crust of toast into her mouth. "At least, that's what I'm always telling the girls."

"You're not yourself." He dabbed his mouth with a napkin and tossed it onto his empty plate. "I've known you long enough to spot the signs. Something's up, and it's doing your head in."

Rachel gave him a faint smile. "Tired, that's all. When we've cracked this one, I'll take some time off."

"At the rate we're going, that could be a while."

"Do you ever get pissed off with the job, Elwyn?" Why the hell had she asked him that?

"You mean, really pissed off?"

Rachel shrugged, wishing she'd kept her mouth shut. "Just ignore me. I'm being a right mardy cow." She had another go at smiling.

"I wouldn't ditch this job for the world," said Elwyn. "I enjoy myself too much." He gave a light laugh. "What brought that on? And don't joke it away. You meant every word. So, come on, what's it all about?"

It was truth time, well as much as she dare tell him. "I feel at odds with the job right now. I can't get anything right, even Harding is watching me. In fact, it's so bad that I'm thinking of jacking it in."

Elwyn looked utterly shocked. Rachel didn't wait for the inevitable lecture. She got to her feet, leaving him sitting at the table. What she'd said hadn't been a total lie. It had been on her mind all night, and on the way in this morning. It was one way to solve her problems. Leave, and Jed would have no hold over her. He'd probably lose interest.

Back in the incident room, the team were hard at it. "We're waiting on forensics for the shooting, ma'am," Jonny said.

"I'm trying to find out who the third and fourth numbers on Frodsham's mobile belong to," Amy said. "One was Greyson, the other Alice, but there's a third one that he called several times in the days leading up to his murder. The fourth, he rang at least once a day." She looked at Rachel and pulled a face. "I have tried ringing it, ma'am, but there's no answer."

"Good one, Amy. Keep at it. Jot it down for me, will you?" Rachel took the scrap of paper and put it in her jeans pocket. She'd check later whether it had anything to do with Jed.

"Oliver Frodsham had an argument with Greyson, and now both of them are dead. According to the watchman, Croft, Oliver was hired to steal some documents. What if Oliver couldn't get them, and the people who'd asked for them went there last night and did the job themselves?" Rachel said.

"You're talking about Liam Beatty?" Elwyn asked.

"Yes."

"He was brought in yesterday and interviewed." Elwyn went to his desk and found the transcript. "He denied knowing Croft, said he never went to his house. He also denied arranging for his people to visit Croft and threaten him."

"Does he have an alibi? Can he tell us what he's been up to all week?"

"Collecting rents for his boss, McAteer. Who as you know, owns half this city," Elwyn said. "The problem is, we don't have anything specific. Croft was vague about the visits. It didn't take long for Beatty's brief to drive a horse and cart through our argument, and he walked."

That was more or less what Jed had said. "In other words, Beatty would have been free last night to sort out Greyson?"

"Yes, but we'll need evidence," Elwyn said. "Something more than simply wanting to pin this on him."

"The two murders are connected. I want you," she looked at the team, "to find that connection. The argument between Oliver and Greyson. The nuts and bolts from Greyson's warehouse found at the scene. It adds up to more than just coincidence."

Rachel heard the phone ringing in her office.

It was Jason Fox. "We found plenty of prints but none that match anyone of interest, I'm afraid."

"By that you mean Beatty and his cronies?"

"Yes, Rachel. As you would expect, we found prints belonging to Greyson and the secretary. As for the rest, the odds are that they belong to the workforce. We're still looking, so there might be others. Sorry not to be of much help."

"Thanks, Jason, but we should have known. The people we're dealing with are too clever to leave prints behind. What about CCTV?"

"Out of action. It doesn't seem to have been tampered with. It was simply switched off."

Rachel put the phone down. Was Jed behind Greyson's killing? Did he want that piece of land? She could theorise for days. No, there was a quicker way to find out. She would simply ask him.

She took her mobile from her jacket pocket and noticed that she'd missed a text from Mia. Jed had rung and confirmed the cinema for the weekend. Rachel was furious. He had no right. She wanted to find him, have it out, but she couldn't do that. Before the day was out, she could be arresting half his men.

It was lunchtime. She rang Mia at school. "Don't make arrangements for this weekend, I've got plans," she said.

"What about Uncle Jed? And what do I tell Ella? She's looking forward to seeing the film."

"I'll organise something for the pair of you. Don't fret about that now."

"Do I tell him?"

"No, I'll give him a ring myself. He'll understand, Mia. You mustn't worry."

Rachel knew her daughter would be disappointed. Jed was new in her life, exciting, and happy to spend money on her.

"Do you want his special number?"

Rachel inhaled. *Special number?* "Yes, love, that's an idea."

Mia told her and Rachel scribbled it down. It was familiar. She took the note from her pocket. The number Amy was checking. It was the same one. This was the third number Oliver had been ringing before his murder. This proved that Jed knew the lad.

CHAPTER TWENTY-NINE

A quick check in the mirror. During the last few days, the man had become obsessed with his appearance. He was dating again, so he wanted to impress. His hair had been carefully styled by an expensive barber, the recently grown facial hair was looking good and his wardrobe had been given a long overdue facelift.

It was early afternoon, and Luke would be waiting. His day off, he'd said. Perfect for a meet up in town and a glass or two of wine.

The man smoothed his hair, straightened his tie, and licked his lips. The last time they'd met, Luke had given every indication of being interested. The coy looks, the smiles — and that goodbye kiss. The man had savoured that. A new victim, a new chapter. He couldn't wait. Today, he would get it all right. When he had his ultimate victim lined up, everything must go like clockwork, down to the final second. He'd get one go, there'd be no second chances.

There'd been very little about the case in the papers. The police must be tearing their hair out. He smiled. Exactly what he wanted. It was all set up to confuse them even more. By the time he'd finished, they wouldn't know which way to turn.

* * *

Luke was waiting for him at 'their table,' as the man called it. He was confident that this time he'd be less nervous. Luke was the perfect victim, mild-mannered and far too trusting for his own good. Now that they'd met at last, Luke would be much more relaxed.

"I got us a bottle of red," Luke said. "I remembered you saying you liked it."

With a smile and a nod of approval, the man sat down. "I'm glad you came. I did wonder. People often let me down."

"It was good of you to choose me. I've been on that site for weeks but no one has shown any interest," Luke admitted.

"I find that hard to believe."

"It's true. A friend of mine says it's because I don't flower things up. Apparently, I need to show off more, exaggerate a little on my profile. But I can't. I am how I am. No amount of touching up is going to change that."

"I like you as you are." The man took hold of Luke's hand across the table. "As far as I'm concerned, you're perfect. This friend of yours — an ex-lover perhaps?"

Luke shook those lovely curls. "No, a woman. I find women easier to confide in. They understand me. If you do consider dumping me, warn me first, won't you?" He fluttered his eyelashes. "Don't just send a text, please."

"That won't happen," the man said. "I don't have your number for starters." He laughed and after a brief hesitation, Luke joined in.

"Pass me your mobile, I'll give it to you." The man watched Luke tap the number in. "Go on, text me, and then I'll have yours."

The man replied with a kiss and a smiley face. "Do you want to eat?" he asked.

"Yes, I'd like that very much."

"Be a love, pop inside and ask for some menus, and see if there are any spare tables. It's a little chilly out here. I just felt my mobile vibrate. A pain, but I'd better see who wants me."

Luke did as he was told without hesitation. Instead of his phone, the man took a small vial of Rohypnol from his pocket and emptied it into Luke's wine. *Not long now.* A shiver of excitement ran down his spine. Yes, he'd chosen well. Luke was an innocent fool, deserved all that was coming to him. He h*a*dn't intended to go for the kill today, but the way he felt . . . Why not? His gear was all ready and at the house. He'd drug Luke and walk him to the venue. A little fun, and then he'd see.

"I'm sorry, Luke. There's been an emergency at work. They want me to go in." The man held up his mobile. "You can't get away from them, bloody things make it too easy." The look of disappointment on the young man's face was truly touching.

"That's too bad. But there'll be another time. Won't there? You do want to see me again, don't you?"

"Of course. But we don't have to go just yet. Sit down, finish your drink."

"I'd hate it if this ended before we even got started. I do want to get to know you better." Luke downed his drink in one.

The man stood up. "This has nothing to do with us or our developing relationship. It's a glitch, that's all. We'll get it together soon, never fear."

Luke nodded. "I'm so relieved you feel that way. Let's make it this week sometime."

The man put his arm around Luke's shoulder and gave him a kiss on his cheek. "I didn't bring my car into town. I'll have to get the train from Piccadilly. Walk with me," he said. "We'll arrange our next meet on the way." Luke struggled to his feet, already unsteady. The man held him tight as he stumbled. "No worries, I've got you."

Luke giggled. "I must have drunk more of the wine than I thought."

"I know a short cut. Soon have us there."

"This isn't usual for me. I feel funny, my head's all woozy." Luke tripped on the cobbles, almost falling.

"Whoops, old son." A passer-by was showing an interest, and the man dipped his head.

"Is he okay? I'm a nurse," the stranger said.

Just his luck. And it had all been going so well. The man laughed. "Too much wine. I'll get him home, don't worry. He'll be fine."

With a shake of his head, the nurse went. Hopefully, the interfering bastard hadn't looked too closely. The man didn't want a photofit appearing in the dailies. Someone who knew him might see it, and his cover would be blown.

After a ten-minute walk, they were in the deserted street. The man had already chosen a house. The front door was unlocked and there was still the odd piece of furniture inside, including a beaten-up sofa. He laid Luke down on it. This was going to be good.

CHAPTER THIRTY

It was wrestle-with-her-conscience time. Should Rachel tell the team what she knew? She sat at her desk, head in her hands. Tell, and she'd risk her career. Rachel would have to admit to knowing McAteer. How else could she explain having his number? And it wouldn't just be her. Mia would be questioned, all of them would. But keep quiet and she'd be going against everything she believed in.

Dare she question Jed herself? Have a quiet chat about Oliver? Ask him outright what he'd hired him for, and what had happened to the lad? That might be the only way to go. But if Jed had had Oliver killed, he was hardly likely to admit it.

In the meantime, Amy mustn't make further progress with her investigations. The young woman needed something else to occupy her. Rachel returned to the incident room.

"Amy, drop that. Chase up ownership of that land. If we haven't heard back from the land registry, get on the phone. If that fails, get onto the council. They should know."

"Will do. I'll start right away."

Rachel looked at Elwyn. "The Greyson killing. Speak to the workforce again. Dig deep. They've had time to think by now. Someone might have remembered something. Bring Croft in and let's have another word. Ask him if he knows why the CCTV was turned off last night. Ring Mrs Andrews, find out if she's ready to talk to us yet." She checked the clock. "I have to go out. I'll be back within the hour."

Without any further explanation, Rachel grabbed her jacket and left the station. Outside in the privacy of her car, she rang Jed. "We need to talk."

"I knew you'd come round. The girl wants me in her life."

"This isn't about Mia. Meet me now. The pub at the end of Deansgate in ten." Rachel knew that Jed had an office in Spinningfields, so that was doable.

"Fortunately, I'm in town," he said. "But I don't have long."

"Just be there. And it'll take as long as it needs. You're damn lucky you're not being arrested as we speak!"

Wasn't that the truth? If it was anyone but Jed, that's exactly what would have happened. But there was a limit to how long she could cover for him. Suddenly Rachel felt sick. Was that what she was doing? Covering for Jed McAteer? How could she be so stupid? If any of her colleagues got so much as a whiff of this, she'd be out on her ear.

Rachel left her car in the underground car park and walked to the pub. They'd met there in the past. He was sitting in a window seat. She gestured to a table against the wall, in the shadows. She didn't want anyone seeing them.

"What's troubling you, babe?" He got up and pecked her cheek.

"You are. You and your antics." They sat down. "Do you know a young man called Oliver Frodsham?"

Jed shook his head. "Should I?"

"He's been murdered. For several days before it happened, he'd been calling your number. The same one you gave to Mia. Don't muck me about, I want the truth, Jed. Now!"

She didn't like the way he looked at her. No one in the world dare speak to Jed McAteer this way. For a moment,

Rachel thought he might lash out. But he simply inhaled, slowly.

"I'm a lot of things, Rachel, as well you know. But I don't lie to close friends and family."

"I'm neither," she said firmly.

"Family, I think. After all, Mia's my daughter."

She ignored that. "You hired Frodsham to take paperwork from Paul Greyson's office."

"Not me, not this time. And who the hell is Paul Greyson?"

"How can you sit there and tell me bare-faced lies! You know well enough." She was angry now, no longer afraid. He'd tell the truth, or she'd drag him down to the station. "We have statements." She was thinking about what Croft had told them.

He took a mobile from his jacket pocket. "Calls, you say. Look at this." He brought up his call history and showed her. "Unknown number. Calls I didn't answer. Check. Go on," he pushed the phone toward her.

Rachel looked closely. The number that had called Jed did belong to Frodsham. "Where did he get your number from?"

"It's my work mobile. It's on all my business cards." He smiled. "Someone has had a bloody good go at setting me up."

Now she didn't know what to think.

"Liam told me what you did, the interrogation. What was the idea?"

"The land between Piccadilly station and the canal, and adjacent to Greyson's yard. What's your interest in it?"

"None whatsoever. I know of it, it's my business, and I heard it was up for sale. Hugo Franklin must have finally decided to sell."

"Franklin, the developer?"

"That's him. But he'll have a job offloading that little lot. It's too pricy, particularly given its problems."

"What problems?"

"It's heavily contaminated from the old dyeworks. Franklin bought it for a song years ago. Once it's cleaned up, it'll be a valuable site, but the costs are too much for me."

Jason Fox had said there were traces of arsenic on the nuts and bolts they'd found. "Would arsenic be one of the contaminants?" she asked.

"Among other things," he said.

"And Hugo Franklin owns the land? And he knows about the problems?"

"Yes, he is bound to. I did some checking. The records are all there, and as my people will tell you, that particular fly in the ointment was never sorted. Whoever buys it will have the added expense of decontaminating it before it can be built on."

"You're not involved? Not even as an investor?"

"No. Like I said, too expensive. Apart from anything else, it's in the wrong part of the city for me. I'm looking at a site down by the Quays. That'll give a much better return. But not a word. The land hasn't hit the market yet."

Very candid, but could she believe him? "Frodsham is dead, murdered. And so is Greyson." Rachel watched him for a reaction. Nothing, not a flicker.

"I don't know who they are. Nothing to do with me, Rachel."

"Frodsham was a student and Greyson owned a firm adjacent to the land in question."

"Sounds like he should have chosen his friends more carefully."

"What do you mean?"

"The land you're on about. Perhaps you should ask yourself if Franklin was trying to offload and who to. Even contaminated land has a value."

"But it couldn't be built on?" Rachel queried.

"No, there's no hiding the fact. It would come up in the searches. But Franklin is not all he seems. He has a past you know nothing about and a lot of dodgy friends. He may want rid and was pressuring this Greyson to buy. Greyson said no and it got him killed. You need to speak to the owner, Hugo Franklin. Find out from him what's going on."

Rachel didn't know whether to believe Jed or not. "Greyson was found with a bullet through his heart. His office was raided and we found prints. Can you assure me that none of them will belong to you or your thugs?" "I don't employ thugs."

"You employ Beatty. What do you call him?"

His eyes narrowed. "Why are you doing this, Rachel? Why pursue me like I am some sort of vicious killer?"

"Because you are, Jed. You didn't see what was done to Frodsham. Or perhaps you did. Perhaps you were there. What I don't understand is why the torture, why the burning?"

He looked genuinely puzzled. "I have no idea what you're on about. You know my history. Sure, I'm not whiter than white, but I've never killed anybody."

"Because you pay people to do it for you."

"Even if that was true, which it isn't, the usual way is a bullet, not what you're describing."

The problem was, Jed was right.

CHAPTER THIRTY-ONE

Rachel returned to the station, still thinking about whether she believed Jed. He was a good liar. But there was something about the way he'd looked at her that rang true.

"Jason Fox has been on," Jonny told her as soon as she walked in. "Reckons it's urgent, something you'll want to hear."

"I know who owns that land," she told them before disappearing into her office. "Bloke called Hugo Franklin. What do we know about him?"

Rachel called Jason. She needed all the help he could give her.

"Firstly, I took a sample of the blood we found at Greyson's," he told her. "The blood someone used to write those letters on the tarmac."

Mac. She knew that name, and it sent shivers down her spine. Jed's criminal associates always referred to him as Mac.

"What about it?"

"Everything checked out. It was Greyson's blood. Given the trace we found on the nuts and bolts, I took soil samples from the land. It is heavily contaminated."

"Yes, so I've been told. I'm currently trying to work out what that had to do with the deaths, if anything."

"Getting back to Greyson," Jason said. "A message written in his own blood has to be significant. Mac for McAteer is what I'm thinking. Thought you should know."

Those warning bells were back. Jed had just assured her it had nothing to do with him. Besides, he was with Mia and Ella last night. But he did have people on his payroll. One of them perhaps?

"It could be a ploy. Supposing the real killer wants us to think it's McAteer?" It was a stab in the dark, but it was all she could think of. Rachel was desperate for the spotlight to fall anywhere else but on Jed. "Thanks, Jason, I'll get on with it."

She flopped back into her chair. Something weird was going on, that was for sure. None of Jed's people would leave such a brazen clue. They'd do everything they could to cover their tracks. A rival gang? Possibly. But gangsters had better methods of sorting their arguments.

Rachel returned to the incident room but said nothing about the conversation with Jason.

"Did you bring Croft in?" she asked Amy.

"Yeah, he's drinking coffee in a soft interview room, boring some poor uniform to death."

"What about Franklin? Have you looked him up?"

"I can't find anything on him, ma'am, other than a speeding offence. I'm trying to contact him but he's out of town until tomorrow. His secretary will ring me when he gets back."

She needed to speak to Franklin. Only he could clear up the question of the land. Meanwhile, she had to find out if Jed was involved in the two deaths, as much for her own peace of mind as anything else.

"Mrs Andrews? What about her?"

"She's still sedated. Her sister is with her, and she says perhaps later today."

Rachel nodded. "Get me photos of Beatty, McAteer, as many of his people as you can, Frodsham and a handful of randoms. Elwyn, you can join me on this one."

CHAPTER THIRTY-TWO

"What's going on, Rachel?" Elwyn said. "You disappear without saying where you're going, return in a state . . . and what did Jason Fox say to you? You're as white as a sheet. Look, your hands are shaking."

"I'm tired, that's all."

She glanced at him. The look on his face said it all. He didn't believe a word. The urge to confide in him was getting stronger. At least he'd get off her back then.

"It's more than that. Your stress goes way beyond this case. It's a tough one and it's getting to us all, but what's going on with you is off the scale. Tell me. I can help."

"No, you can't." Her tone meant back off. "We have to do this right. I have questions for Croft. Let him do the talking, Elwyn. Don't help him in any way."

Now he was completely lost. "You can't think Croft's part of this?" he said.

"Not knowingly, but he is a vital part of the solution."

"What are all those photos about? What are you trying to prove?"

She had no answer for him. What she was 'trying to prove,' as Elwyn put it, was whether Jed was a murderer. Croft could hold the key.

Douglas Croft was chatting to his family liaison officer. He looked up when the two detectives entered the interview room and sat down facing him. "Is it sorted? Can I go home?"

"Soon, Mr Croft. I've got one or two questions for you, if you don't mind."

He looked fearful. "Won't put me in danger, will it? Those thugs will kill me if I say the wrong thing."

Rachel smiled. "All I want you to do is look at some photos and tell me who you recognise."

Rachel hoped she was on the right track. Part of her believed what Jed had told her this afternoon, and part of her wanted to believe it. She took out the photos and selected one of the randoms.

"Have a look at these photos and tell us if you recognise anyone. There's no rush. Just take your time and tell me if any of these men ever came to your house. What about him?" She placed the image of the random on the table.

Croft studied it intently. "No. I already told you — it was Liam Beatty who threatened me."

She put two more in front of him.

He shook his head. "Neither of them."

"You're doing fine, Mr Croft. Now let's try a different approach, concentrate on picking out the men you do recognise. What about this one?" She put down one of Oliver Frodsham.

"I know him. That's the lad who broke in. The one I wasn't supposed to mention."

Rachel nodded, that was what she expected. "And him?" The next photo showed Beatty. It was a good, clear one. If Croft had ever seen the villain then he'd recognise him from this.

"No. Never seen him before."

Rachel closed her eyes momentarily. So far, so good.

"Do you know Liam Beatty, Mr Croft? Have you ever met him?" Elwyn asked.

"Well, no. Not a crowd I mix with," Croft said. "Far too dangerous. I know the name though, everyone does. Anyway, he told me who he was loud enough. I'm surprised the neighbours didn't hear. He shook his fist in my face, telling me what'd happen if I let him down."

"You see, Mr Croft, that gives us a problem," Rachel explained. "You can't be sure it really was Beatty, and neither can we."

She sifted through the remaining photos and put some down on the table, face up, as if for a card trick. They were all known associates of Jed's, including one of him. "Take a real good look and tell me if you see the man who came to your house and threatened you."

Croft pondered the photos. He seemed to spend hours looking at each one. To Rachel, every moment was a lifetime. It was a simple enough task. He should have picked out anyone he recognised immediately. But, apart from Frodsham, he knew none of them. So it couldn't have been Beatty or anyone connected to Jed who went to Croft's house that night. That was the only explanation.

"Mr Croft, this," she tapped the photo, "is Liam Beatty. Since you tell me you've never seen this man, I have to presume that whoever threatened you was using his name, pretending to be him."

"It certainly wasn't him," he said. "He isn't bad-looking. The bloke I met were an ugly bugger. Nasty too."

"Would you be prepared to describe this individual to one of my officers so we can try and get a photofit?"

"If it helps." He looked at her, relief written all over his face. "Does this mean those mean bastards aren't after me — that McAteer bloke and his mob?"

"Yes, it does, Mr Croft." Rachel smiled. Little did Croft know that she was just as relieved as him.

CHAPTER THIRTY-THREE

Rachel returned to the incident room to be told that Mrs Andrews was waiting downstairs. "She reckons she's feeling okay now and wants to talk while it's still fresh in her memory," Amy said.

"Okay. You can join me, Amy."

Despite what she'd told Amy, Agnes Andrews looked tired and drawn, and was obviously still shaken. She sat on a sofa in the soft interview room, clasping and unclasping her hands.

Rachel smiled at her. "Thanks for coming in, Mrs Andrews. It was a dreadful ordeal you went through last night. We do need your input, but only if you are up to it."

"It's best if I do this now. Get it over with and I'll be able to rest." She wiped her eyes. "That man killed him, didn't he? I heard the shot. I was terrified. I should have done something, but I just froze, I couldn't think straight. I hid under the desk in Paul's office, praying that lunatic didn't come after me."

"You rang us, and that was the right thing to do," Rachel said gently. "Are you able to describe this man to us?"

Agnes shook her head. "It was too dark, he was wearing a hoodie and he kept to the shadows. He knew Paul's name.

I got the impression they'd spoken before, that Paul knew him."

"What did he want?" Amy asked.

"He kept going on about some report he thought Paul had. He'd paid some young lad to break in and steal it, but the lad didn't hand it over. He accused Paul of knowing about the land next door and how contaminated it was. He said the documents he wanted were about the land being cleaned and okay to develop." She cleared her throat and took a sip of water. "It didn't make much sense to me. It's all rubbish. There never was any report, and everyone connected to that land knows about its problems. He said that Paul was involved in some scam, but I know he wasn't. Paul was as straight as they come. The man said the land would be sold cheap and everyone would keep quiet because they were being paid to let everything go through."

"Did this man mention anyone by name?"

"No. He referred to them as the boss and his business partner. And that they wouldn't be happy if they didn't get the report. Paul asked if it was a man called McAteer who'd sent him."

Rachel's heart sank. Was this right, or was someone trying to fit Jed up? Either way, it was bad news.

"Did he threaten you, Mrs Andrews?"

"Not really. Before he shot Paul, he told me to go to the office and get the money we keep in the safe. I think he wanted me out of the way." She sobbed and dabbed at her eyes. "He could easily have killed me too. Got rid of the pair of us."

She was right. Rachel had to consider why he hadn't. The only reason she could think of was because he wanted Mrs Andrews to pass on this tale about the land, the report, and the person Paul Greyson had accused of being involved in the scam to buy it cheap and develop it, Jed McAteer.

"Are you sure this man didn't mention any names himself?" Rachel asked.

Mrs Andrews nodded. "No, it was Paul who asked about McAteer being involved."

"And he alleged that they know the truth about the land?"

"That's the impression I got," Mrs Andrews said. "But you must understand how scared I was. I couldn't concentrate properly."

Rachel smiled at her. "You've done very well. If there's anything else you think of in the coming days, please get in touch."

Amy showed the woman out. Rachel sat on for a few minutes, deliberating on what she'd heard. Jed had assured her that he had nothing to do with the land. If what Mrs Andrews had just told them about a 'boss' was true, he could have been lying. Nonetheless, she couldn't bring him in and ask him. Better to go a different route and lean on Franklin, the owner. Find out what he had to say about the land and what his plans were for it.

CHAPTER THIRTY-FOUR

Luke had no idea what had happened. The last thing he remembered was drinking on Canal Street with James. Now his head hurt and he couldn't move his arms and legs.

"Sorry old son, but it has to be tonight. I've no patience you see, can't wait any longer."

As Luke became more aware he realised he was lying naked and bound on an old sofa. He was terrified. "What are you doing?"

"Calm down. I need to get ready."

"I want some water, please I'm dying of thirst."

"Shut it! You'll have to wait."

He had no choice. Luke watched as James went through some ritual of getting dressed in weird-looking clothing. First, a white disposable coverall that covered him from head to toe, including his hair. Next a face mask, and finally, goggles to protect his eyes.

"Water. Please." Luke's eyes were wide open now and watching James intently. The sudden change in events was mind-boggling. "What are you doing? Why the fancy dress?"

"Drug wearing off? I can fix that." James smiled wickedly. "I bet you don't remember, do you? I slipped you something when we were at the pub."

"Why do that? I was happy to come with you."

James laughed. "This get-up I'm wearing is for you, pretty lad. We're going to make a night of it."

This was madness. "I don't feel well. I want to go."

"I bet you do," James said. "There is real fear in those baby blue eyes. So touching. And so reminiscent of someone else. I should feel pity for you, for what I'm about to do. But I don't." He leaned forward until his face was almost touching Luke's. "You look like the man I hate most in the world. You are so like him when he was younger, it makes me sick."

"That's not my fault," Luke said hastily.

"I know that, I'm not stupid. But nonetheless you will suffer, just like the first one. And I'll enjoy watching you."

Luke could see from the crazed look on the man's face that he meant it. "You're bloody mad! Let me go or I'll scream the place down."

The man smiled cruelly. "No one will hear you. The street is full of empty houses. I'm going to hurt you and very soon you're going to die in agony. I hope that has sunk in."

"Give me some water, please," Luke asked again.

"You can have some water, but I have laced it with the drug I gave you earlier. Still want some?" He gave the young man another cruel smile.

"Let me go," Luke begged. "You know this is wrong. I'm not the man you hate. Why not go after him instead?"

"Oh, I will, but not yet."

James crossed the room to a table and searched through a bag of tools. This was Luke's only chance. His wrists were bound with rope, but he had skinny arms and delicate fingers. If he wriggled and pulled enough, he might work them free. While James hummed tunelessly and picked out some knives from his bag, Luke quickly worked on the rope.

James returned to Luke's side, a smile on his face. "Still want that drink?" The man put a cup to his lips. "Now drink. You'll feel better. It'll take the edge off."

This was it. His hands were raw and bleeding, but finally free. Luke jumped up and knocked the cup into the air. He gripped James by the throat and squeezed. "Let me go or I'll fucking throttle you!"

Luke saw his confusion. James obviously didn't have a plan for victims who fought back. Luke's ankles were still bound but his arms were free.

"Slim little hands they might be, but they're strong." Luke smiled. "Worth their weight in gold, don't you think?" James had a knife in his hand, but was too shocked to stop Luke from snatching it and cutting the rope round his ankles. "I should slit you open for doing this to me," Luke said, putting the knife to the man's throat.

Tear rolled down James' cheeks. He was genuinely afraid. "You trapped me. You're just like him. You always come out on top."

"I've no idea what you're on about. You're mad. Who always comes out on top? We only met a few days ago," Luke said.

"But I know you — ever since I was a child, you've tormented me. I suffered at your hands. I was screaming, burning, and you did nothing to help. You watched my skin blister and laughed, you cruel bastard! Getting even with you is the only thing that has kept me going all these years. That's what drives me — revenge."

Luke shook his head. "Not me. You're off your head."

* * *

The man was stunned. This wasn't like him. For a moment, he'd lost it.

"I'm not mad, just damaged." The man shook his head, trying to clear it. This wasn't the person who'd hurt him. It had been another pretty, blond boy, many years ago. But Luke was here now, and he would suffer for it.

"Help me, Luke. Help me find a way back. I don't want to be like this for the rest of my life." The man had to redress the balance, regain the upper hand, show this upstart who was the real boss. He'd have to appeal to the gentle Luke, the one he'd first met. The one he could exploit.

The man wiped the tears from his face. "Let's start again. I'm truly sorry for this. I don't know what came over me."

Luke looked as if he was having none of it, but he asked, "What made you like this? What happened back then?"

The man hoped Luke was wavering.

"Release me, and I'll show you." The man held his breath. This had to work. Luke could do him a lot of damage. "I have an older brother," he began. "A beautiful creature, the favoured child, but he hated me, made my life miserable. I told my parents, but they didn't believe me. In their eyes, my brother was a prince who could do no wrong. I was nothing but an ugly boy who couldn't make friends."

"That must have been hard," Luke said. "It's never good to live in someone's shadow."

"It was worse than that. I lived in fear of my life."

"Couldn't anyone help you? A relative? Family friend?"

"My brother was crafty. No one ever witnessed his acts of cruelty. Then, one day he delivered the blow that left me like this. We were on holiday, camping miles from anywhere on the Isle of Mull in Scotland. Our parents had gone to the nearest town to get food. They were gone hours. My brother had been teasing me, threatening to hurt me. He chased me through the woods, but I hid. I can still recall those tree roots I took shelter in. They scratched my legs and ripped my clothes." The man stood up. "I can't say any more. It's too painful."

"Have it your own way. But unless you unload, no one can help you."

"Let me show you, you'll understand then." With Luke still holding the knife, the man slowly removed the coverall. Underneath he was wearing a T-shirt and jeans. He pulled the T-shirt over his head and showed Luke his naked torso. Luke winced.

"My brother eventually found my hiding place. He dragged me back to the caravan and threw me into the camp fire like I was nothing but a piece of rubbish. As you can see from my body, the burns were horrific. It took hours for help to arrive. I was in such agony that I lost consciousness. Now, every time I look in the mirror, the scars remind me of what he did."

"Wasn't he ever punished?"

"No. I was too traumatised to tell anyone. I couldn't talk for weeks. When I did eventually tell them, my parents didn't believe me. They said I was a liar and took my brother's part. He told them I'd been mucking about and slipped. They thought he was a hero for pulling me out."

CHAPTER THIRTY-FIVE

"What was that business with Croft all about?" Elwyn asked Rachel on their way back to the incident room.

"Just getting things straight," Rachel said. "I know it's late, but gather the troops. I need a word."

Rachel first went to her office. She needed a moment. That had been hard. If Croft had pointed the finger at Beatty, it would have been game over. But he hadn't, so she was able to fight on. It was true Mrs Andrews had put McAteer in the frame, but only as much as Greyson's killer had spoken about him. That was a long way from being proof. She took a few deep breaths. Time to speak to the team. She grabbed her notes and joined them.

"It is my opinion that we have been deliberately manipulated," she began. The team whispered among themselves. "Douglas Croft was certain it was Beatty who threatened him. That, combined with the alleged battle over that land, meant that we believed him. Mistake!"

The whispering stopped.

"What Croft didn't say, and it's our fault for not making sure, was that he'd never actually met Beatty, or even seen him." Amy gasped. "We have just shown him photos of

Beatty and McAteer. No reaction, nothing. Not even a hint of recognition."

There, she'd said it. Jed's name had passed her lips in front of the team and her world hadn't come to an end.

"Someone as yet unknown planned the Frodsham and Greyson murders and wanted to make them look like they were the work of McAteer and his gang." This was chancing it. After what Mrs Andrews had said, she just hoped she was right.

They looked at each other, stunned.

"Do we have any clue who it was?" asked Jonny.

"No, but Croft is doing a photofit of the man who visited him. He has to be significant, otherwise why bribe Frodsham to steal those plans? And don't forget, Greyson himself denied any plans existed. Not that we took much notice at the time. Greyson's killer didn't harm Mrs Andrews. I think he wanted her to tell us her story, name people, divert suspicion."

"What made you suspect Croft had got it wrong?" Elwyn asked.

"Gut instinct," she lied.

"And why rule out McAteer?" he said. "In my book he fits the bill."

"It's the land. McAteer would know that it's contaminated. He's been in the development business long enough. He buys land on prime sites, ones with no complications. He'd have no reason to risk good money on something that needs that much work. We'll interview Franklin. He's a developer as well as being the owner of that land. We'll ask him if he has any idea why there's been all the interest."

Elwyn was still doubtful. "Why would the killer go to so much trouble to lead us astray like that? We were all set to lay the blame on McAteer and his thugs. And in my book, that's what we should do."

"You're wrong," Rachel said. "That's exactly what the killer wants. He's hoping we'll stick the lot on McAteer."

"But why?" Elwyn asked.

Rachel shrugged. "We don't know what is going on inside the killer's mind. We don't even know who he is yet."

"That leaves us back at square one." Elwyn scratched his head. "What about that piece of land? Does it have anything to do with the murders?"

"Who knows?" Rachel said. "But I doubt it. Someone went to a lot of trouble to make it look like it did. They even invented a tale about stolen documents, and got Frodsham to watch the place."

"But why did Greyson have to die?" asked Elwyn.

"We were supposed to chalk that one up to McAteer, presume it was him who wanted the land. After what we've just learned from Croft, we know that isn't true. The killer has tried very hard to cover his tracks. We now have to work out just who the intended victim was — Frodsham or Greyson. The Greyson murder sent us down the wrong trail, blaming McAteer and his mob. And I think that was deliberate."

"What do we do now, ma'am?" asked Jonny.

"We go back. We look at Oliver Frodsham's life again and we tear it apart until we find something."

"I thought we'd done that," Amy said sullenly. "He was just a kid, a gay student doing a bit of moonlighting on the side."

"There has to be something, Amy, or he wouldn't be dead. We also look at Croft. I want a forensic team at his home. I want the neighbours interviewed. Someone may have seen his visitor. We need a description of the man who threatened him that night."

CHAPTER THIRTY-SIX

It had gone horribly wrong. They weren't supposed to fight back. The last one hadn't. So much for going easy on the drugs. The man was angry with himself. He could not afford such mistakes with the next victim. That would be his brother and when he did him, it had to go like clockwork.

He took a last look around the room. There was blood everywhere, even up the walls. Luke had bled like a pig. Served him right. In a tender moment, when he'd made Luke feel sorry for him, the man had slit his carotid artery with a very sharp little knife he kept in his back pocket. The look on Luke's face had been priceless! Well, he shouldn't have got him to talk. Putting him through all that angst about the past had been a mistake.

No time to tidy up. He'd heard noises outside and earlier someone had banged on the door. Fire was not only part of the ritual but it was also a great cleanser, destroying any forensic evidence. A can of petrol was ready in the boot of his car, which was parked up a couple of streets away. His tools were stashed in the sports bag and ready to go. With luck he could have this wrapped up within fifteen minutes or so, and be on his way.

He was closing the front door when a voice rang out. "You can't doss down in there, mate. This lot's coming down tomorrow!"

Now he'd been seen. Nothing was going right tonight. The man pulled up the hood of his coat and shuffled off without saying a word.

"Bloody cheek! Get down the hostel on Baltic Street if you want a bed for the night. Come back here and I'll have you carted off by the law."

Why couldn't people mind their own business? He didn't ask much. All he wanted was to be left in peace, to get on with what he had to do. He'd no idea this street was patrolled. That must have been what all the noise had been about earlier. He should have thought of that. When he got to a corner, the man risked a look back. The street was empty. Fortunately, the interfering bastard hadn't gone into the house.

Soon he was back with the petrol. He was running out of time. There had been calls from home, which he'd ignored. Once inside, he sloshed the fluid about. The last bit in the can he reserved for Luke.

"Goodbye, old son. Sorry it ended so abruptly. You shouldn't have crossed me. That way you would have gone in the canal. Too late now. This'll have to do."

He poured the remaining fluid over the lower half of the body, trying to avoid the face. He lit a rag and threw it at the sofa. The place was ablaze in seconds.

He legged it down the road, but his bad luck persisted. He could hear people shouting after him. He took a quick look back and saw a couple of blokes outside the house, one of them already on his mobile. He hoped that the body was burned to a crisp before the fire brigade got there. It had been a desperate measure. He just hoped he would get away with it.

CHAPTER THIRTY-SEVEN

It was late, and the team had had enough. Croft had only got so far with the photofit and would return in the morning. She'd arranged with Jason Fox for a team to go to Croft's house. Now that they had ruled out any connection with Jed, they badly needed a break in the case.

Rachel made for home. All she wanted was a big glass of wine and a long soak in a hot bath. The last thing she needed was a domestic drama, but that's what was waiting for her.

Rachel was hardly through the front door when a tearful Mia greeted her. "Tell him, Mum!" Mia said. "He's been giving me the third degree. Says I'm not to see him again. Wants his number too. He'll spoil everything, like he always does."

"Calm down," Rachel said, dumping her briefcase in the hall. Alan was in the kitchen, pacing up and down. Always a bad sign.

"Before you start, he's harmless." she called to him. Not strictly true, but he wouldn't harm Mia. Megan was sitting at the table looking smug. "Is this down to you?" Rachel challenged. "Is this what I get for tackling those idiots you brought to the house last night?"

Rachel had had enough. She could do without Alan wading in and asking questions she couldn't answer. "I'm going upstairs for a bath. It's been a bad day. This case I'm working on is getting to me and the team, it's dead end after dead end. It's late and I'm far too tired to argue with you lot!"

"There she goes. Things get tricky at home, and she plays the work card. You're so predictable, Mum," Megan said.

"Watch the lip, young lady," Rachel warned her eldest.

Finally Alan got a word in. "Come on then, who is he? He takes our daughter out but I've never even heard of him. Not from you or from these two, until this week."

What a sheltered life Alan led! Most of Manchester knew Jed McAteer's name.

"He's no one, just a friend," she lied.

"He said he was my uncle. Your brother," Mia levelled at Alan.

"Well, he's not. I don't have a brother, as you all well know."

Rachel had had it. "Can we leave this until tomorrow? I'm too tired to do this now. I told you, he's a friend. Jed doesn't have much experience with kids, so he thought it better to pass himself off as a relative. A bad idea, I agree, but he wasn't thinking."

"So he's your latest boyfriend? Is that it?" Alan had his hands on his hips, a look of distaste on his face.

"Okay. Yes, he's my boyfriend. Happy now!" Rachel thrust her face close to Alan's. "Bowling and a bite to eat. A couple of hours. Not kidnap or worse. You might not know him, but I do. You need to grow up, Alan, and stop being so jealous!"

Rachel stormed off up the stairs. This was down to Megan. She was stirring it, no doubt in a fit of pique about Alan throwing her friends out of the house. That girl needed a serious word! Rachel was just stepping into the bath when her mobile rang. It was Elwyn. Was there no end to this?

"What now?" She barked, grabbing a towel. "Can't you give me a break? I hope this is important and not about the bloody stuff you want to stash. If it is, you can do one! I've just about had it with other people's problems. I've had an ear bashing from Alan I could have done without, and want some peace!"

The line had gone quiet. Rachel could hear her own rapid breathing. She needed to calm down. She'd just blasted Elwyn for no reason, which wasn't like her.

"It's work, ma'am," he said coldly. "A fire in town, and there's a body. This one does look like the Frodsham murder."

Not again! Rachel asked for the details and ended the call. So much for a quiet night.

CHAPTER THIRTY-EIGHT

Rachel pulled out of the drive, filled with guilt. Why had she behaved like that? Poor Elwyn. He, of all people, didn't deserve it. She was a crap boss. To make matters worse, he wouldn't complain, he never did. All she wanted was a night off, to be left alone to do some serious thinking. Now that Alan knew about him, Jed had become an even bigger problem, and she needed a solution quick. But none of that was Elwyn's fault. He was simply the wrong man, at the wrong time.

The murder had taken place in a dingy back street in Ancoats. Most of the houses were boarded up. Signs at both ends of the street proclaimed it as part of the regeneration of that part of the city. Great if it came to pass, but the state of the place indicated that the houses had been left to go to ruin for some time.

She ducked in under the tape. "We were lucky," said a fireman standing by the door. "We received a call and got here quickly. We're only up the road."

"Can I go inside?" Rachel asked, wriggling into a coverall.

"Yes, but one of us will come with you. And you wear this." He handed her a hard hat. "There's not a lot of fire damage, but the property itself is unsafe."

Elwyn came up to join her.

"You too? What do we look like?" she said.

"Not a fashion parade is it, ma'am? It's a serious business. Another murder, very like the first."

His tone made her wince. Well, she deserved it. "Look, I'm sorry. I shouldn't have barked at you like that. You've no idea what I walked into at home. They haven't got a clue, the bloody lot of them."

Elwyn sniffed and walked in ahead of her. Great! Now he had the sulks too.

Butterfield was bending over the body. "The legs and torso have been badly damaged by the fire, but not the face or hair."

"Are forensics in with a chance this time?" Rachel asked Jason Fox.

"Yes. Look at that." He pointed to a petrol can. "Our killer left it behind, as well as this." He picked up the remnants of a white coverall similar to theirs. "With luck we might even get DNA."

"Sorry, only just got the message." A panting Jonny Farrell came up behind them. "I was in one of the bars up town and didn't hear my phone."

Rachel said nothing. She'd upset one of her officers tonight. No way was she going for the full set. She'd already noticed that Amy was missing and decided to let that go too.

"Much like the last one." She nodded. "This confirms it. We can forget all the other angles we've explored. We've got a serial killer on our hands."

Elwyn was listening but not Jonny. He was staring at the body. "I've seen him somewhere," he mused. "I'm just not sure where."

Rachel was suddenly alert. This was important. "Try and remember," she urged. "Was it recently, part of this enquiry?"

"Can I take him away?" Butterfield asked.

"Give us a minute," Rachel said. "Jonny, the chances are he's gay like Oliver. Think about the people you spoke to, the places you went."

"Sorry ma'am. I know I've seen him recently but I just can't think where. I go to a lot of the bars in town."

"Okay. Perhaps we should all go and get some sleep. Although I think that aspect of my life is currently cursed."

She looked at Elwyn, who was making for the front door. He'd said very little. Rachel needed a word.

"I'm a cow," she said, catching up with him. "You shouldn't get the sharp end of my bad day. It wasn't fair. All I can offer, Elwyn, is a heartfelt apology."

"You're doing it again, blaming the job. But it's not that, is it?" He sounded angry. "Something's eating you and it's personal. I don't expect you to share everything with me. But this is affecting your work, Rachel, how you go about it. We see things most folk never see. We deal with stuff like that in there all the time. We should talk, share, not clam up and suffer, and then take it out on the team."

He was spot on. But Rachel still couldn't tell him about McAteer. That would just about finish everything.

"You've got this wrong, Elwyn. I'm tired, exhausted even. That's all it is. It's certainly nothing you've done. You are great to work with—"

"I've remembered, ma'am!" Jonny Farrell ran up behind them. "Canal Street, that day I was asking questions about Frodsham. He was there, waiting for someone."

CHAPTER THIRTY-NINE

Friday

The following morning, the team assembled in the incident room. Rachel was in early and had already updated the board.

"Jonny," she said, "I hope you've given our latest victim some thought overnight. I want a statement from you. And, please, make sure you put in as much detail as you can recall. Anything and everything is important at this stage."

"We have the photofit, ma'am," Elwyn said. "It's a little odd. Whether it's Croft's faulty memory or our killer really does look this strange, I'm not sure, but it's all we've got."

"Let's have a look."

Elwyn passed it over. "He's a weird one, alright. Interesting haircut and a lot of facial hair. That makes it difficult." Rachel handed it to Jonny. "You said our latest victim was meeting someone. Take a look."

They waited while DC Jonny Farrell squinted at the image, frowning. Finally, he nodded. "I think it's him. But when I saw him he was dressed up, and his hair was sorted. I remember the tash and the beard though. We spoke briefly. I showed him the photo of Frodsham, and he said he couldn't help. He suggested I ask in the bars." Jonny looked round at the others. "He saw I was nervous, and told me not to be. That was when our victim turned up and sat down at the table." He paused, considering this. "I got the impression it was a first meeting. This guy," he waved the photofit, "had a rose in his lapel. And before he came up to the table, our victim had been looking around."

"That's good, Jonny. First meeting, arranged previously, perhaps through a dating site. See if you can find out." She turned to Amy. "Check missing persons. We might strike lucky this time."

"Wasn't there anything in that house that might give us an identity?" Elwyn asked.

"Nothing yet," she said, "but I'll speak to Jason shortly. See what forensics turned up."

"PM?" he asked.

"We're waiting for the nod from Butterfield."

The meeting broke up. Elwyn followed her into her office.

"Want a cuppa?" she offered.

"I'd prefer the truth. You've changed over the last few days. I reckon something's happened and it's knocked everything haywire."

Very perceptive. "No, you're wrong. A good night's sleep and I'll be fine. Are you up for the PM?"

He nodded and left, obviously unhappy with her explanation. There was nothing Rachel could do about it. She picked up the phone and called Jason.

"Got anything from last night? A wallet perhaps, or something to help with an identity?"

"I'm afraid not. The fire didn't do that much damage, but the victim's clothing was burnt. We're dredging through the remains to see if there's any trace of a wallet or bank cards, but nothing yet. It's possible that the killer took them."

"We are really pushed on this one. We need a break. All the other leads have gone nowhere. Effectively, we're starting again. Anything you think might help, no matter how small, let me know at once."

Rachel checked the system for the reports that had come through this morning. There was a statement from the man who'd seen the killer on the street and shouted after him. His description was too vague — jeans and a hoodie and carrying a sports bag. How many people in Manchester looked like that?

She returned to the incident room. Jonny was busy scrutinising the dating websites and Amy was on the phone. There was no sign of Elwyn.

"There's a woman downstairs, ma'am," Amy told her. "She's asked to talk to someone about a missing person. She told the desk sergeant that she might know the unidentified victim from last night."

CHAPTER FORTY

Rachel had the woman shown up to one of the soft interview rooms and went with Amy to meet her. The woman was in her forties, dressed for work in a suit and carrying a briefcase.

"My name is Marian Shaw," she said. "I'm sorry to be a bother, but I heard on the news about the fire last night and the body you found. I was immediately concerned. You see, my brother, Luke, didn't come home. He didn't text or phone either, which is not like him at all."

"And you don't think he stayed with a friend? Had a bit too much to drink and slept over? Perhaps he's gone away for a few days," Amy said.

"No." Marian Shaw shook her head firmly. "It doesn't work like that with Luke and me. He's a very quiet young man. He trusts me, tells me everything and we text constantly when he's not at home. This is totally out of character. Something is wrong, I just feel it."

"Does he live with you?" asked Rachel

"Yes. Luke is twenty years younger than me, and although he's an adult, I feel responsible for him. He's delicate, gets emotional. He wouldn't survive five minutes on his own. We share a flat in Didsbury. There's just me and him. Our parents are gone."

Rachel frowned. "I appreciate that you're worried, but it isn't much to go on. Like my colleague said, there could be a whole host of explanations."

"If he planned to stay out, then he'd phone me." Marian seemed absolutely certain about that. "He left the house late yesterday afternoon for a date with a man he'd met recently on Canal Street. Luke is gay and doesn't have much luck with his love life. I have no idea how he first met this man either. He wouldn't give me a straight answer. I have a feeling it was on a dating site. He's barely been off his laptop recently."

That set the alarm bells ringing.

"Did he talk about this man?" Rachel asked.

"Not much. He did tell me that his name was James and that he was older than him. Luke is twenty-five."

"Was that all he said?"

"Yes, and I wasn't happy. I take an interest in Luke's friends and he's usually quite open, but he was particularly cagey about this one. When I heard about the fire, and the body being found, I was worried."

"Did Luke have any friends who were still at uni?" Rachel asked.

"No, they weren't his type."

"You're sure? He never mentioned a young man called Oliver Frodsham?" It occurred to Rachel that the victims might have known each other.

"No, that's not a name I recognise. Mostly Luke kept himself to himself. He had a few close friends and didn't stray much outside the group. Which is why this sudden online dating surprised me."

"What made you think the body we found might be your brother?" Amy asked. "No details have been released yet."

"As I said, he didn't come home, and he hasn't contacted me. I've been ringing his mobile all night but got nowhere. Half the night it went to voicemail and then it went dead. He's never done that before. I had to come here this morning, to make sure, put my mind at rest. I brought this."

She handed Rachel a photo.

Rachel swallowed. Would this nightmare never end? It was their victim. She passed it to Amy. "You're right, there was a suspicious death last night, and as yet the person involved hasn't been formally identified. I'm afraid the photo you just showed us does resemble the body we found. Would you be prepared to take a look? See if it's your brother, Luke?"

"Yes, that's why I'm here," she said in a tight voice. "Do we do this now?"

Rachel nodded. The woman appeared collected, even unemotional, but that could be a front. If this was her brother, then who knew how she'd react? "My colleague here will take you. If it is Luke, we will have to get a statement from you. In the meantime, if there is anything else you recall about the man he met, please do let us know. We will also need Luke's laptop. Amy here will accompany you back to your home to collect it once you're done."

CHAPTER FORTY-ONE

A couple of hours later, Rachel was in front of the team again. "We have an identity for last night's victim. He is Luke Shaw, aged twenty-five. Obviously not the footballer of the same name. Forensics are at his home collecting certain belongings of his. I'm hoping his laptop proves useful. His sister thinks he might have met his killer online."

"If he did, we'll have a profile and image for the killer, ma'am," Jonny said.

"If that's how they did meet, I'm hoping the site was a paid one and that our killer used his bank card. That would tie it up nicely, wouldn't it?" She smiled.

"And if he didn't?" Elwyn said. "We might get a lead on our killer, but we're still short on evidence."

Rachel looked at Amy. "Get his phone records. Let's see who he contacted recently. Forensics are still going over the first kill site, now we have a second, and Douglas Croft's house. They are bound to come up with something."

"What if they don't?" Elwyn said. "This guy is obviously very clever. He's covered his tracks — except for this last time, of course."

Rachel looked around at the others. "Elwyn has a point. Our killer can't have been aware that the street was patrolled.

The men who chased the killer off were employees of the firm hired to do the demolition. Given the number of rough sleepers in Manchester, their job was to ensure the buildings were empty. Being disturbed rattled him. The killer had to make a quick exit and left a right mess behind. If we're lucky, that'll be his undoing. I think that everything we picked up after that first one was deliberately left for us to find. The bolts led us to Greyson, for example. That started an entire train of investigation that led nowhere."

"DCI King." Harding had come in unnoticed. "Give the photofit to the press. The local paper reckon they can get it on the front page of the evening edition."

"Flush him out?" Rachel asked.

"Either him or those close to him," Harding said. "Now that we have a likeness, we must prevent any more killings. I'm sure you agree." With a meaningful look at Rachel, he strode out.

"Okay. Jonny, give a copy of the photofit to the press office so they can get on with it."

"Why those particular victims, I wonder?" Elwyn said. "Were they chosen at random or for a particular reason?"

"I'd say random," Jonny said. "Anyone the killer could dupe."

Elwyn shook his head. "That's not how I see it."

Rachel looked at him. "You have a theory, Elwyn?"

"Frodsham and Shaw look very similar. Surely, the rest of you have noticed? Young, smooth skinned and blond. Look at the face shape, the eyes. Our killer is choosy, and I for one would like to know why."

"Perhaps they're simply his type," Amy said.

"Greyson doesn't fit the profile," Rachel added.

"Greyson was killed to throw us off the scent. And that's something else. The killer knew about Beatty and McAteer. He'd done his research."

"What are you getting at?" asked Rachel.

"Only that he must have spoken to people, asked about the villains. He even impersonated Beatty. I'd like to find out who he got his information from."

Elwyn had a point. "You think he mixes with them?"

"Who knows?" Elwyn said. "But in any case, he knew their names and reputations. He also knew about that land. I'll have a discreet word with one or two people. See what turns up."

"Would you do that quickly, please? They may have a name, a description, something we can use." Elwyn nodded. "Amy, make sure you get that meeting with Franklin as soon as you can. I'll join you. We need to know if anyone asked him about the land in the last few weeks."

Meeting over, Elwyn disappeared through the office door. No smile, no words of encouragement. He was still upset, and that made her uneasy.

No time to dwell on it now. She had a text from Megan. Alice Brough's father was home. Rachel had asked Megan to let her know when he showed his face. She'd have to fit in a visit.

CHAPTER FORTY-TWO

All night, and into the next day, he kept going over and over what had happened with Luke. His mistakes plagued him. It had been stupid to assume that his victims wouldn't retaliate. After all, they were fighting for their lives. But he'd never have thought the mild-mannered Luke had it in him.

The man sat on a garden chair in the early afternoon sunshine, and went through it all again, moment by moment. He stopped at the point where Luke grabbed him by the throat. It had thrown him, making it necessary to deviate from his plan. He wasn't good at improvising.

The fire had been discovered almost at once, and no doubt had been extinguished promptly. They would have Luke's body. But what else had he left behind? Some of his gear, but not the most important items.

Wracking his brain looking for mistakes wasn't helping. The man needed to do something about his predicament. He must find out for sure what the police had, and what they would do next. If there was nothing in the local press, there was someone he could ask as a last resort.

Picking up his coat, he left the house. He'd been holding his breath all day, waiting for the news to be reported, but there was nothing. A few words on the radio about the fire and that a body had been found, but nothing more. In that case, he could be worrying unnecessarily. He smiled. To date the police had followed the false trail he'd laid for them. Dare he believe that he'd done it again, run rings around the bloody lot of them, and this time without even trying?

But his luck was about to run out. In the corner shop, he saw the photofit image on the front page of a daily newspaper. It was more a caricature than a likeness, but nonetheless, get rid of the beard and messy hairstyle and it looked like him. Where in hell's name had they got that from? This was where he lived. Anyone from round here would be able to recognise him. He tucked the paper under his arm and walked out, hearing the shop owner shouting after him. In his panic, he'd forgotten to pay.

The man did what he always did at such moments. He caught the first train into town and made for Canal Street. He found an empty table in one of the bars and scoured the paper. The police were asking for anyone who recognised the man in the picture to ring a number they'd given. They even had his name. Luke Shaw had lived with his sister in Didsbury. It must have been her who'd gone to the police and reported him missing.

He had to think. Had he slipped up? He must have done. If only he could remember where. He'd been in one helluva hurry, but he'd made sure to take everything that might tie him to the lad, including his mobile phone and clothing. He looked at the likeness again. Who had given that to the police? He must have been seen.

This had to stop. He had to find a way to throw them off the scent. Give them something else to think about. But how? The article didn't give the name of the officer in charge, but the man knew very well who it was. Greyson had told him before he shot him. A certain detective was interested, a female one.

He had a shrewd idea who the female detective was. If he was right, she was a woman with a family, and that made her vulnerable. But could he be sure it was her? He would check. There was someone he could ask. If he was right, then there was plenty of scope to wreak havoc. It was risky, he'd prefer not to, but what choice did he have? Everything could go pear-shaped in the blink of an eye if he did nothing.

His stomach was churning. He ordered a whisky and took out his mobile. A quick call home, put their mind at ease. He'd be late back and didn't want to cause undue worry.

CHAPTER FORTY-THREE

The team were all dog tired, so Rachel told them to call it a day. The last week had been relentless. She sat down at her desk. She was weary herself, but she still had the reports and statements to plough through. There might be something that had been missed, and she was desperate for a break. But the print swam in front of her eyes. It was no good, she needed a diversion. Rachel picked up the phone and called Jason Fox.

"I want a favour," she began. "I need to know if any twins were born on a particular date in the maternity unit at Stockport hospital. Can you do that?"

"Why not ask them yourself?"

"Come on, Jason, you know what it's like. If I get a doctor who's a stickler for the rules, it'll take a court order before we get anything." She paused. "You know people, Jason. It's nothing dodgy, but it would help me clear something up."

"Is it related to the case?"

"In a roundabout way. It came about because of Oliver Frodsham's murder. We interviewed a student called Alice Brough who, coincidentally, is a friend of my Megan's. This Alice told me she has a twin brother, Alfie. According to Alice, he disappeared when they were children. But her father insists he never existed. I find the whole thing very odd. She has shown me evidence — a birth certificate and photo of them together."

"That doesn't make sense. Why would the father do that?"

"Alice put two and two together and made five. It's a pretty far out theory and I'd like to know if there's any possibility of it being true. Please, Jason. Just this once."

"You owe me one," he said, "alright? And I won't forget."

"No problem."

"But I've a meeting to go to first. I'll make a few phone calls after that and text you."

"Thanks, Jason. How's the forensics coming on?"

"I was going to ring you, as it happens. We're still working on the items we've collected, but Frodsham's mobile is interesting. We found his prints and DNA, as you would expect, and prints from the homeless gentleman who handed it in. But there were also prints and traces of DNA from one other person. I've run them through the database, and there is no match."

"Thanks, Jason. Let me know the minute you find anything else."

They knew that Frodsham used the mobile to contact only certain people. That fourth person must have been important. It was a puzzle that Rachel would have to work on. Another mystery was what had happened to it after the killing. It was possible the killer had taken Frodsham's belongings, but not the mobile. John Jones, the homeless man, had used it and handed it in. The only explanation she could think of was that the killer had lost or forgotten about the mobile. Given what was on it, there was no way the killer would want it found. Rachel wondered how Jones had got hold of it. Perhaps he'd stolen it, thinking it was valuable. There'd have been time when the killer left the arch to dump Frodsham's body in the canal. If that was the case, did the killer realise it was missing?

Rachel made a note to check with John Jones the next morning. If she could find him.

Amy knocked on her door. "Ma'am, Hugo Franklin is able to see us this evening. He's currently in a meeting but will meet us at his office in town once he's free."

"I thought I told you to go home," Rachel said.

"He's a hard man to pin down. I rang on the off-chance and bingo." Amy smiled.

Rachel could have done without it tonight. The day had been bad enough. "Okay. But we go straight home afterwards, agreed?"

"I'm quite happy to go alone, ma'am. I'll take a uniformed officer with me." This surprised Rachel. It wasn't like Amy to volunteer to do anything.

"I appreciate that. It's getting late and I could do with getting home. You know about the contamination. Here's the forensic report on the soil samples." She handed Amy the document. "We want to know what Franklin has planned for that land, if anything. Get the measure of the man. Report back in the morning."

Amy nodded. Rachel regarded her for a moment. "You're alright with this? No other pressing engagement?"

"No, ma'am. I rang his secretary and got a positive response, that's all."

CHAPTER FORTY-FOUR

Amy Metcalfe was determined to get her act together. She'd seen the way Jonny worked. He was keen and good at the job. If she wasn't careful, he'd be the one moving up the ladder, not her. Doing the donkey work, helping the boss tie up loose ends would certainly help.

Speaking to Franklin was a start. She'd never met the man, and apart from what she'd read in the press, she knew nothing about him. But he was *the* person in Manchester to go to if you were interested in anything to do with housing or land.

Amy was shown up to his office. He was waiting for her, a tray of coffee at the ready.

He waved her over to a chair. "I'm sorry you've had to wait so long. Some of these meetings go on for hours, and I've been out of the area for the last couple of days. So, what have I done to attract the attention of the police?" He gave her a tentative smile.

"Nothing, I hope." She smiled back. "We'd just like your input in a case we're investigating. It concerns a piece of land between the railway arches by Piccadilly and the canal. We'd like to know what you have planned for it."

"Ah yes. 'Weaver's Croft,' as it was once known." He took a file from a pile on his desk and opened it at a map. "The mills have gone now, in particular the spinning mill. It was replaced in the twenties, but that one has now fallen into disrepair as well." He smiled. "We've been dancing around this stretch of land for years, so it's still untouched."

"Are there any plans to sell it?"

"That would be tricky for the buyer. That's why it's still undeveloped. The land is heavily contaminated from the old dyeworks that operated alongside the spinning mill. Whoever bought the land would have to pay to have it cleaned up, and that would be expensive."

A perfectly straightforward answer, no attempt to dodge it. No conspiracy there then. "Has anyone shown any interest at all?" Amy asked.

"A few developers over the years, but as soon as we put them in the picture they backed off. Money is tight and there are better sites available within the city boundaries."

"Are you aware that there's a rumour circulating that a report has been produced stating that the land has been cleaned up and is fine?"

He laughed. "Nonsense! Now that would put me on the wrong side of the law." He regarded Amy and the uniformed officer for a moment. "Am I allowed to know who's spreading this rumour?"

"We don't know ourselves, to be perfectly honest."

His mouth pulled into a thin line. "When you do, I'd like to know. I might sue."

She nodded. "I'd like a list of all interested parties, please."

"I'll get my secretary to sort that for you in the morning. Why is this land so important?"

"A young man was murdered there recently. His body was thrown into the canal. We were misled into thinking the land was related to the murder, and that it was about to be sold."

Franklin shook his head. "How sad. I don't recall us being contacted. I take it your people did search the area for clues or whatever?"

"Yes sir, but we had a little difficulty finding out who owned the land. We put in a request to the land registry but it took a while."

"I see."

"Can you think of anyone who would want to make you look like the bad guy in this? Perhaps make out that you had produced a report stating that the land had been cleaned up and was ready to market?"

Franklin shrugged. "I have enemies, of course. Business rivals. If that's what's happened, it could be any of them."

"Have you upset anyone in particular who you think might go to these lengths to blacken your name?"

"That's quite a question. No, I can't."

"Do you know a man called McAteer?" Amy asked.

"Not personally, but I know the name." He frowned. "Has he shown an interest in the land?"

"As far as I'm aware, none whatsoever." Franklin appeared to be genuinely surprised at the question. "I'll organise that list of interested parties for you, but I can tell you now, it numbers no more than three or four. And McAteer doesn't figure. Was it him that spread the rumour about the land?"

"We don't think so. You see, there was a second death," she said. "The owner of a business next to Weaver's Croft was murdered. We thought that his murder had something to do with his property adjoining the land. Whoever was buying wanted the entire plot if the sale was to be concluded."

Franklin's eyes narrowed. "That's rubbish."

"Did you know the victim? The owner of that business? His name was Paul Greyson."

"No," he said abruptly. "I'm sorry, I can't help and I'm pushed for time. I've told you all I know. If people have been killed because of that land, I've no idea why. It is unlikely to be redeveloped anytime soon."

Why had he suddenly become flustered? Amy couldn't think what she'd said that might have touched a nerve. Wait! The mention of Greyson's name. That's what did it.

She smiled and stood up. "I think I've got everything I need. If I have any more questions, I'll be in touch."

On her way back to the car park, Amy thought about what Franklin had told her. Nothing she could use, that was for sure. At first, he'd given the impression of being above board and eager to help. Then, when she mentioned Greyson, his whole demeanour had changed. Amy wasn't sure what that meant but, as DCI King would say, her gut instinct was tingling. Thinking like a detective. It was a new experience for the DC.

CHAPTER FORTY-FIVE

Saturday

He was right. Rachel King was the investigating officer for the case, and the man knew exactly where the King family lived. Couldn't have been easier. From his car parked outside, he could see that DCI King's vehicle was gone. A workaholic that one, according to rumour. The curtains were open and a young teenage girl was standing at the window, looking at him. He ran a hand through his hair and waved. Mustn't frighten her. Time to make his move.

The girl had obviously seen him walk up the drive, but made no move to open the door. But after a few rings of the bell, there she was. "Mia, isn't it?" He gave her a friendly smile. "I was hoping for a word with your mother. It's not usual for me to bother people at the weekend, but this is important." The charm offensive usually worked. "Is she in?"

The girl barely lifted her face from the mobile she was clutching. "She's out, and so is Megan. You'll have to come back." A pause. "I can't let you in, there's no one here."

His heart leapt, couldn't be better. "What a shame. She'll want to speak to me. It's regarding a case she's working on. I have some information, and I know it will be useful."

"I'll tell her. Mum'll ring you when she comes back."

"Okay, but you need my details. New phone, hence a new number." He smiled. "I've got a card in the car with everything on it." The man walked back towards his vehicle. As he hoped, the stupid girl was following. Not a care in the world or a thought in her head, other than the phone.

The man leant in from the passenger door and felt around in the glove box. "Well I thought I had . . . sorry about this. I won't keep you."

But the girl wasn't listening. She still had her eyes fixed firmly on her mobile. She was giggling at an image. Time to strike.

The man stood up and darted round behind the girl. He struck the back of her head with a metal torch taken from the glovebox. She collapsed like a sack of potatoes. Snatching the phone from her hand, he threw it in the gutter. It took only seconds to manhandle her into the passenger seat.

Bingo! He had what he needed — leverage.

Within hours, the police would be aware that she was missing. The search for him would be forgotten. They wouldn't have the time. All officers and resources would be thrown at finding Rachel King's kid.

He took a quick look round. No one about. Apart from a farm across the road, this was an isolated spot. No nosey neighbours staring out of bedroom windows, no twitching curtains. Time to go, and then let events play out. On the way out here, the man had thought very carefully about where to keep the girl. He had the perfect place. She was his ace in the hole. Should anything go wrong, the blame would fall elsewhere.

* * *

No one liked working over the weekend, including Rachel, but it couldn't be helped. She was at her desk early. Next to show was Jonny Farrell. He put the kettle on and asked if she wanted a brew.

"Anything come through from Shaw's laptop?" she asked him.

He was studying his computer screen intently. "Just checking the reports. Ma'am, the payment for that dating site was made with Frodsham's debit card."

Rachel groaned. She should have seen that one coming. The killer must have found it on Oliver and decided it would be useful. "Anything else?"

"IT Forensics are still working on the laptop, but they have sent through a report about the dating site. It was a bona fide site, nothing unusual or fishy. Shaw contacted a number of young men and they all check out, apart from one." He passed her a printout.

"This is a dead ringer for the photofit. This is our man." But did it help? Looking at the image, she could see it was heavily photoshopped. This wasn't what their killer really looked like.

Jonny put a mug of tea on her desk. "They may find more. You know, emails and the like."

"I doubt it. Our killer wouldn't be so stupid." She took a sip of her tea. "This isn't bad." Jonny had cottoned on fast to how she liked her brew. A large mug, no sugar, and strong. Builder's tea, her father used to call it.

Amy was next to arrive. "Franklin knows all about the contamination and was happy to talk about it," she said. "But when I mentioned Greyson's name he suddenly got shifty. I thought I'd do a little research, see if they knew each other. Franklin said not, but you never know."

The three of them got busy and the morning rolled on. No sign of Elwyn. He knew how important it was to get on top of the case, so where was he? If it wasn't for their spat and the way he was behaving, Rachel would have simply rung him at home. Oh, why did men have to be so difficult?

Her mobile beeped. It was Megan, and she sounded concerned.

"Mum, do you know where Mia is? She was supposed to go round to Ella's but she never turned up. I've been to Dad's and she's not there either."

"Have you rung her?"

"Her phone must be turned off."

Alarm bells. "And you've tried everyone? Did Ella say if they were meeting anyone else?"

"No, they planned to go swimming, then afterwards Ella's mum was making lunch."

"Okay, leave it with me. I'll phone as soon as I've found her."

Rachel had a good idea what had happened, and she was livid. Jed McAteer! Not happy with what she'd said the other night, he'd obviously taken matters into his own hands and picked Mia up for that day out anyway. He had no right.

She rang his mobile. "Bring her home now!" she shouted as soon as he answered. "What do you think you're doing?"

"Rachel?" He sounded only half awake. "Sorry, I was asleep. I've been up half the night travelling. What's the matter?"

Her stomach lurched. "She's . . . not with you?" Her nerves were jangling. Her voice shook. "You're sure? You haven't seen Mia today?"

"No. I haven't seen her since the other night. You made your feelings quite clear. I'm not a moron, you know, despite what you think."

Rachel ended the call, her head spinning, frantically searching her mind for some logical explanation.

CHAPTER FORTY-SIX

Rachel spent the next ten minutes ringing as many of Mia's friends as she had numbers for. None of them had seen her. When she'd left for work this morning, the kids had still been in bed. Rachel had looked in on them both as she always did. Whatever had happened took place between seven and . . . what time was it? Nearly eleven thirty.

Rachel rang Megan back. "When did you last see Mia?" Silence. "Come on, Meggy This is vital."

"I'm trying to think, Mum. I left the house at nine and went for a run. I bumped into Alice and we had a coffee at that new place in the village. I didn't get back until ten minutes ago."

That narrowed it down to just over two hours. "Was Mia up when you left?"

"She was getting some cereal. She'd just done her injection."

That was something at least. "Have a look round. See if she left a note and then ring me back."

Rachel was going quietly mad. She had an urge to dash out into the main office and tell the team, get their help, and organise a proper search. But if Mia was genuinely missing, there was no way she'd be allowed to be involved.

"Sorry I'm late. I've been talking to some interesting people at the betting shop on Market Street."

It was Elwyn, and the smile was back on his face. He meant that he'd been talking to an informer. But Rachel couldn't answer. She managed a half-hearted nod and then burst into tears. The story came out garbled and didn't make much sense, but Elwyn got the gist.

"Megan is sure?" he asked.

Rachel nodded. "She's looking around the house, to see if Mia left a note. But that's not how it works. She'd have rung me first, told me if she was going out."

"I'll get out there, have a look around. You should go home. I can take you with me. Jonny can follow in your car. You're not going to be much use here."

"What about the case? We've still a long way to go," she said.

"Forget about it, we'll carry on."

She sniffed. "I should make an official report, at least tell Harding."

"I'll sort all that once we're sure Mia is missing. I mightn't have teenage girls myself, but I do have nieces. They run rings around my sister. She's constantly on their backs for not keeping her in the loop. This could all be a huge misunderstanding, you know. Are you sure she didn't say anything about going out today? You've been so busy with the case you might have forgotten."

"I don't slip up like that with Mia," Rachel sobbed. "Because of her diabetes I have to know where she is at all times. We've worked out a routine over the years. She knows I stress, and does her best not to worry me."

"Get your stuff. We'll leave right away." Elwyn went into the main office to have a word with the team.

Rachel sighed. She couldn't think properly. Everything seemed unreal. She couldn't believe this was happening.

Her mobile rang. It was Megan.

"There's no sign of a note, Mum." She paused and Rachel heard her take a breath. "But I found Mia's phone in the gutter outside the house. She must have dropped it because the glass is smashed."

That did not sound good. Mia would never just drop her phone and leave it lying somewhere. Was it possible that she'd been snatched? Had the phone been dropped in a scuffle? "Leave it now, Meggy. The forensic team will want to see it." For a few seconds, the professional in her overrode the mother. "Lock the house and go round to your dad's. I'll be home soon." One daughter was missing, she had to ensure the other was safe. Now for the tricky bit. Rachel tapped in Alan's number.

"Have you seen Mia this morning. Is she with you?" She held her breath, let there be a simple end to this. But he hadn't, in fact he still sounded half asleep. "She's missing." Stark but effective, now she had his full attention.

"She said nothing to me about going out. Does this have anything to do with you?"

"I don't know. But in case it does the investigations have started. Keep Meggy with you. I'm on my way."

Rachel finished the call before Alan had a chance to ask anything more. Her mobile rang again. It was Jed. "Have you found her?"

"No. I'm going home. I'll ask the neighbours across at the farm if they saw anything."

"When we met the other day, you mentioned Franklin. Everyone thinks of him as a respectable developer, but he's a crook. Get in his way once and you don't get the chance to do so again."

"That sounds scarily like you, Jed."

"I'm serious, Rachel. Cross him at your peril. Have your team had any contact with him?"

"He was interviewed yesterday."

"He won't like it. You may have stumbled on something he'd rather stayed hidden. Let me in. Tell me what you're investigating and I'll help. At least I can rule people out."

"There's no way I can do that," Rachel said.
"Never mind the protocol. Our daughter is missing."
"You think I don't know that? I'm not stupid!" She ended the call, grabbed her stuff and went to find Elwyn.

CHAPTER FORTY-SEVEN

The timing wasn't ideal, but he had no choice. It had to be now. After the debacle with Luke, he didn't have much time left. At this time of day, the target would be at his desk. A phone call, a few chosen words and the man would lure him to his death.

Everything was ready. He'd prepared as well as he could. He would have one chance, and one only. Get it wrong and it was game over. This one wasn't like the others. He wouldn't hesitate, he would fight back.

So this was it. This was what it had all been about, all the planning, and the killing. The man he had hated for so many long years had to die, and only then could he find rest. This was the final chapter, and his excitement was building. Hidden in the shadows of the workshop, he could hear his own heart thudding. The sound threatened to drown out everything else.

The minutes ticked by, and doubts set in. What if his target had been delayed? Changed his mind? This anxiety wasn't good for him. Then the man heard the sound of a car engine. He was here. He took a quick peek through the small window. It had been years since he'd seen him, and now there he was, large as life. Tall, hair still fair, and pristine as ever in a dark suit and smart shoes. As instructed, he'd come alone. Perfect. The man did not want to have to deal with a third party at this stage of his quest.

The target shook the double doors, and their rattle echoed through the workshop. Metal cosh at the ready, the man waited in the shadows.

"You in there?" his brother shouted. "You think I've got nothing better to do? This is way out of order—"

The man struck out, metal hit bone, and the person he'd hated for years crashed to the floor.

"Got you at last, you bastard!" The man grinned. "This is where it ends."

He dragged his brother by the feet to the centre of the space. He'd forgotten what a big man he was, how heavy. He couldn't lift him onto the bench as he'd planned, it would have to be done on the ground. He slashed at his victim's clothes, cut them away, and bound his wrists and ankles tight. The man placed a stool a short distance from his prisoner and sat, gloating over his fallen nemesis. The person who had terrified him for most of his life, the stuff of all his nightmares, was lying naked and bound at his feet. For the first time ever, the man had him at his mercy and not the other way around. He intended to take full advantage of his victory. He would make him suffer, feel real pain. And then he would kill him.

The blow on his head had been enough to knock him out, but he would regain consciousness soon. The man wanted him lucid. He had to know exactly what his fate would be.

"What the hell . . ?" He groaned. "You can't do this to me."

The man laughed. "That's where you're wrong. I can do whatever I want. If I've learned anything these last weeks, it's that I can be in control."

"You're being ridiculous. You don't have it in you. You're a first class wimp, you always were."

The man smashed his brother's shins with the cosh. His brother screamed and swore at him, his face contorted with pain and anger.

"A lot has changed over the years," the man said. "I've changed. I'm not the lad you knew, and now it's time for you to pay for what you did to me."

"What do you think I did to you? You can't possibly remember."

"The fire, the camping trip, I remember that. I've still got the scars."

"We were kids," his brother said. "It was an accident."

"It was no accident. You pushed me into that fire on purpose. You watched me burn and you did nothing."

"I pulled you out! You lived, didn't you?"

"I'm scarred, I tell you, physically and mentally too. You told our parents it was my fault, and they believed you. They always took your side over mine. You could do no wrong in their eyes."

His brother's lip curled. "They were idiots."

"Idiots you wrapped around your little finger. You had the blond hair and the pretty face. Me, I was just a kid with nothing going for him."

"Yeah, yeah, my heart bleeds. Why now? Why all this suddenly? Years have gone by since we were kids. I've not seen you in decades. What's made you feel the need to persecute me now?"

"I want to get even. I need you to pay for the suffering you caused."

"But why now?" his brother asked again.

"Because I'm dying."

CHAPTER FORTY-EIGHT

All the way home, Rachel sat next to Elwyn in silence, hugging her bag for comfort. If anything happened to her precious Mia she couldn't carry on. This was her fault. She'd neglected her family, left them to their own devices. Jed had suggested that Mia's disappearance was linked to the case, and he could be right.

"We'll find her," Elwyn said. "Forensics will be on the job within the hour. Jason is pulling out all the stops. If Mia has been taken, the abductor will have left a trace and Jason will find it."

But would he? They had found nothing so far. Three dead bodies, no motive, no suspects, basically no idea. No trace. And now the worst possible thing had happened. If it was the killer who'd taken her daughter, what did that mean? And why now?

Alan was waiting in the front garden. "What the hell's happened? I can't find any sign of a struggle. Are we sure about this?"

"Have you seen her? Were you even looking?" Rachel flew at him. Why was he never where he should be? He shook his head. "No, I didn't think so! I told you last night I was working most of the weekend. Where were you, Alan?"

"She rang me this morning asking if I'd take her and Ella somewhere. I told her to give me until eleven and then we'd arrange something."

"Did you see anyone come to the house?" she asked.

"No. I've been in the back with Ade for the last hour. He's been measuring up."

"Bloody Ade!" Rachel brushed past him and went inside. The place was much as she'd left it early this morning. Dirty dishes filled the kitchen sink and mugs littered the table top. Mia's room was a mess. Most of her clothes lay scattered across her bed. She obviously hadn't been able to decide what to wear.

Elwyn knocked on the bedroom door. "I've had a quick word with the neighbours."

"We haven't got any," Rachel said. "There's me and Alan and the farm across the road."

"The woman at the farm was hanging her eggs for sale sign on the gate. She saw a red Citroen pass by at about ten thirty. A man was driving and there was someone in the passenger seat, although she couldn't see who."

"Registration plate?"

"No, she didn't look, didn't think it was important."

They heard Jason and his team arrive.

"We'll go next door to Alan's and leave them to it," she told Elwyn. "We'll just be in the way."

She went downstairs. Jason was already examining the front door.

"I'm going on the theory that whoever took your girl knocked on the door or rang this bell." He brushed fingerprint powder over both places. "He could have worn gloves, of course, but it's worth a shot. I'll need to take prints from your family too."

"Anything, Jason. Just call when you're ready."

"I should have some results through later. Might help things along."

"Right now, I'll take anything. This is a nightmare. It's got me climbing the walls." She burst into tears. "Sorry, I don't usually do this, it isn't me." She rubbed her eyes. "It's just the waiting, the not knowing. It's tearing me apart."

"It's your daughter, Rachel. We all understand," Jason said.

Her mobile beeped. It was another call from Jed. Not now, please. She cut him off without answering.

Alan was pacing about. He came over as soon as they went inside. "That man from the other night. Could he have taken her?"

"What man?" Elwyn asked, immediately suspicious.

"No . . . one, just a friend who took Mia and her mate bowling," Rachel said. "He's not in town this weekend anyway."

"A boyfriend?"

Rachel looked at Elwyn. Wasn't she allowed any private life? "No. Just a friend."

"Name?" Elwyn asked. "I'll speak to him anyway, just to rule him out."

"Sorry, I'm going . . . to throw up." Rachel dashed out of the room. This was getting worse by the second. If Alan remembered Jed's name, or Megan told Elwyn, she'd had it. Everything was crashing down around her.

* * *

DC Amy Metcalfe studied the screen in front of her, trying to make sense of what she read.

"How d'you think it's going?" Jonny asked.

"Aren't you supposed to be taking her car to her house? You'd better get going, she might want it," she said.

"Just leaving. I thought I'd have another look through the reports first. Can you imagine having a kid go missing like that? D'you reckon it's got something to do with this little lot?" He nodded at the pile of paperwork on his desk.

But Amy wasn't listening. "I've got an odd one here. It seems our Paul Greyson and his wife used to be foster parents. The records are old and sketchy, but one of the kids he took on had the surname Franklin."

"You're thinking our Franklin? I suppose it might be, but then again it could be someone else entirely."

"If this Franklin is the same man as our developer, then it is significant. I asked him if he knew Greyson and he said he didn't."

"It's a long shot if you ask me. How many Franklins are there around here? Bound to be more than one for sure. And anyway, what reason would he have to lie about knowing Greyson?" Jonny asked.

"Because he has something to hide," Amy said.

"Like what?"

"I've no idea. Could be anything." Amy got up from her desk. "I think I'll go and ask him. If anyone wants me, I'll be at his offices."

"And if he doesn't work weekends?" Jonny shouted after her.

"I'll take my chances," she called over her shoulder.

CHAPTER FORTY-NINE

Hugo Franklin's offices were open, but he wasn't there.

"Mr Franklin received a call and had to leave," a stony-faced receptionist told Amy. "You could try later, although he may go straight home."

"Can I have his home address?" Amy asked.

"We don't give out personal information," the receptionist stated.

"I wouldn't ask, but this is a murder enquiry." Amy showed the receptionist her badge. "You don't want to be had up for obstruction, do you?"

"Here." She handed over a card. "But he won't be there. It's Saturday, he'll be on the golf course."

"Which club?" Amy asked. Why hadn't the woman said so in the first place?

The receptionist pointed it out on a map of the area pinned to the wall. "Didsbury. That's where he lives. The course is there, about half a mile from his home."

Amy set off. It would take her twenty minutes or so to reach the address she'd been given. She'd guessed that Franklin would live somewhere like that. Didsbury was a much sought-after suburb, boasting some of Manchester's largest and most expensive houses. It wasn't that far out of town either, which was an added attraction for a rich local businessman.

As she expected, Franklin lived in some splendour, in a large executive-style residence probably built by his own firm. She parked up on the drive and made for the front door. She rang the bell, knocked on the downstairs windows. No reply, nothing.

"He's not in." The woman's voice came from behind her. "I've called a couple of times and he's never here."

Amy turned and regarded the young woman. "I know you."

"Probably. You're police, aren't you?" She tapped her nose. "I have an instinct for these things."

Amy suddenly twigged. She'd seen the girl's photograph on the incident board at the station. It was Alice Brough.

* * *

"Are you okay? You were deathly white. I thought you were going to faint," Elwyn asked Rachel.

She gave him a wan smile. "What did they say?" She was dreading his reply. If either of them had remembered the name 'Jed,' he'd make the connection and despite what had happened, the third degree would start.

"Nothing. We were too concerned about you. Alan and Megan are outside in the garden. They are distraught about Mia and worrying about you is adding to the pressure."

"Sorry. I don't know what came over me. I'm not as tough as I thought I was. I should be able to work this out, but I can't. It has to have something to do with the case. But I'm damned if I can see what."

"I think you're right. He slipped up with the Shaw killing. He had to make a hurried exit. I think we've found something that has our killer running scared. Taking Mia is his insurance."

"But what do we have, Elwyn? As far as I can make out we've got bugger all."

"I'm trying to work it out. I had a word with an old friend, someone I've got stuff from before. A mine of information, he is. A man was hanging around the clubs and pubs down Cheetham Hill about a month ago asking odd questions. He wanted to know about McAteer and Beatty. How they operate, what they were up to currently. I showed him the photofit and he thinks it was him."

"Did he get anything?"

"He was handing out cash, so, yes, I'd say he got what he needed. Certainly enough to terrify Croft."

"That doesn't surprise me. This man is good at finding what he needs. He knows all about me. He has my name, address and details about my family."

"It wouldn't take a genius to find out who the SIO on the case is, and then to find out one or two personal details. There are plenty of links. Frodsham's Facebook friends for example. We've spoken to them, some know Megan. A few discreet enquiries and he has the lot."

"It's freaking me out. He could have been watching us."

"You okay now?" Alan shouted from the door. "Have you told them? Given them that bloke's details?"

Elwyn looked at her, frowning. She had to come up with something.

"What's going on, Rachel? You're holding something back and I can't work out why. If there is someone who Mia might have gone off with, we need to know. Who is this man Alan is on about?"

"It's not him. We've already spoken. Alan is being dramatic as usual. A friend of mine took the girls out, it was no big deal. But you know how jealous he gets."

"Does this friend have a name? We might as well check him out anyway."

"We've got something!" Jason Fox came over to them, a smile on his face.

Rachel could have kissed him. If ever she needed a break, it was now. And not only that, Jason had diverted everyone's attention from her.

"We did get DNA from an item found at the site of Luke Shaw's killing. The mask he used had saliva traces on it. We've run it through the database and got a familial match."

"Not a direct one?" Rachel asked. "You're saying that our killer hasn't been in bother before, but a close relative has?"

"Yes. The matching individual was pulled over for suspected drink-driving five years ago. He got into a spat with the officer attending to him and ended up being arrested for assault.

"Who is it, Jason?" Elwyn asked.

"Hugo Franklin."

CHAPTER FIFTY

"We'll bring him in," Elwyn said.

"I want to come with you," Rachel said.

"Not a good idea. You're compromised. Stay here. I'll keep you up to date, don't worry."

On his way out of the house, Elwyn collared Jonny Farrell who had just parked Rachel's car on the drive. "We need to speak to Franklin urgently. DNA results show that he's related to the killer. With luck and his help, we should be able to clear this up."

"Amy went off to talk to him earlier. His name came up as a possible foster child of the Greyson's. Mind you, she wasn't sure it was our Franklin."

Elwyn was surprised. "I'd no idea they fostered kids. Ring her, tell her what we now know about the DNA result and ask where he is."

Elwyn presumed that Greyson hadn't mentioned it because, being in his late sixties, his fostering days were well behind him. "I wonder who else he and his wife took in? Ring the office and get Stella to check, will you?"

Elwyn rang Amy and brought her up to speed. "Did you get hold of him?"

"No, sir, he's nowhere to be found. I tried his house and the golf club but he wasn't at either. But I did find Alice Brough lurking around outside Franklin's house, which I find odd. I can't see what the link between them is. It's not in any of the reports. She refused to tell me why she was there, said it was none of my business and went off home."

Elwyn told Jonny, but he didn't have any idea either of what Alice was doing, or what she knew. Elwyn made a mental note to speak to her once they'd found Franklin.

"Stella is doing her best with the fostering records, sir," Jonny said. "But they're not all computerised, so it could take a while. But she did find out something interesting. Greyson also took on Alexander Brough, Alice's father. There's a note on the record. It seems the pair didn't get along and eventually had to be separated. Brough left the Greysons but they kept Franklin."

"We'll ask Alice about that later. Do we have a mobile number for Franklin?" Elwyn asked.

"I'll ring Amy and ask her."

Amy had a mobile number for Franklin but said it was turned off.

"Another dead end." Elwyn threw his hands up. "His office might know. Try them again."

A few minutes later Jonny was still shaking his head. "They've no idea either. The best his secretary could come up with is that he could be lunching somewhere. But there's nothing in the diary. Apparently he got a phone call, left saying he was going out, and that was all."

Elwyn was annoyed and frustrated. "Rachel thinks we've got a lead, that we'll speak to Franklin and get the killer's name. I'm not going to disappoint her. We'll keep trying until we find him. In the meantime, we'll have that word with Alice."

They drove off. Elwyn was disappointed. He wanted to crack this, but more than that, he wanted to help Rachel get her daughter back. He just wished she would tell him what was troubling her.

* * *

Amy went back to the station. Various results had come in while they'd been gone, notably Luke Shaw's mobile phone data. She scanned through the numbers. And there it was. The unknown one from Oliver's phone. Both he and Luke had called it. That meant it had to be significant. It was chancing it, but things were desperate. She picked up the office phone and dialled the number. It was turned off.

She went back to her research. Amy was going with the theory that Greyson and Franklin had known each other. So why had Franklin denied it? From what little information they had, Greyson and his wife had been exemplary foster parents. They'd taken on several children during their time with the agency, some long term.

Amy wanted to know what Franklin was doing in care in the first place. The record, such as it was, said a lot about Greyson but not much about Franklin. She searched for his birth record. It was an unusual name, it should be simple. But after an hour spent scouring every website she could find, there was no sign of him. Hugo Franklin did not seem to exist.

CHAPTER FIFTY-ONE

Rachel couldn't settle. She stood at the kitchen window watching Alan pace up and down in the garden. He was hurting every bit as much as she was. It was a shame that they couldn't offer each other any comfort. But the rift between them had widened recently, particularly since Jed had surfaced again.

Doing nothing didn't suit either of them, but all they could do was wait and watch. It was soul destroying.

"The prints from the door have gone. We'll rush it through. We have prints from the items found at the Luke Shaw kill site to match them against. If the abduction is down to the killer, we'll know soon enough."

Rachel thanked Jason. He was doing his best but what he said terrified her. The man they were hunting was a beast. He'd done horrific things to his victims. The idea that her child had fallen into his hands was unbearable.

"Someone's just pulled up outside in a car I don't recognise," Jason said.

Rachel took a look through the window and her heart sank. Jed. Like she didn't have enough on her plate! She couldn't risk him coming inside. Jason knew of his reputation, and although he worked closeted away in forensics, he might still recognise him.

She marched outside to meet him. "What the hell are you doing here? Don't you think I have enough to worry about without you coming round and causing trouble?"

"Don't start, Rachel. She's my daughter too. I want her found every bit as much as you do."

Rachel got into the passenger seat. "Drive. Get us away from the house before anyone sees us."

"Ashamed of me? That it?"

"Too right I am. You've no right even contacting me, never mind coming to the house."

"I want to find Mia. I take it you've checked that she's not with any of her friends?"

"I'm not stupid, you know."

"You think her disappearance has something to do with the case you're working on?" he asked.

"Yes. But as yet I have no evidence. If forensics do their bit, I will know very soon."

Jed pulled into a layby. "Names, Rachel. Apart from Franklin, who are you interested in?"

"I can't tell you that."

He leaned over, caught her by the hair and yanked her round so she was facing him. Rachel yelped, and her eyes widened in a mix of fear and anger. She knew all about Jed's temper when he didn't get his own way.

"Don't you dare get rough with me!" she said. "It won't work, Jed. I'll have you put away before you know what's hit you."

"I can help," he insisted. "I know people who will talk. Don't be a fool, Rachel. You need me."

She pulled herself free. Rachel wanted to fly at him, pummel him with her fists, but he was right. She swallowed hard. "Two young men, horribly tortured and killed. Both gay. One found in the canal that runs through that land I asked about."

"The other one you mentioned?"

"Greyson. We believe he was killed to throw us off the track. For a while our killer was trying to point the finger at you. Oh, and Hugo Franklin."

"Franklin? I told you, he's not someone you get on the wrong side of. He's a bad bugger."

"That's not how he presents himself. He employs a lot of people in this city. He is building houses all over."

"Underneath that exterior, he's a villain. Franklin is running another, less legal enterprise that he's successfully hidden from the law."

"What enterprise? How come we know nothing about it?"

"Because he pays people to keep quiet. He's secretive. I know for a fact that he's changed his name at least once. Check him out. You'll see. Your team have spoken to him, he'll feel threatened and that makes Franklin dangerous."

Rachel felt her panic rise again. "In that case we need to know who he really is. We have a DNA trace for a member of his family found at one of the murder scenes. That means a close relative of his is our killer."

"I've met him socially, and we've played golf, but never once has he spoken about his family. He isn't married and has no children. That much I can tell you."

"Do you think he could have played a part in this? Could he have been party to the murders and taken Mia?"

"If whatever is going on risks exposing his other business, he would fight dirty to protect his interests. Like I told you, he's a bad one. He's capable of anything."

Rachel rang Elwyn on her mobile.

"Have you found Franklin?" she asked.

"No. We've checked his home and the golf club. His office has no idea where he's gone. Rachel, where are you? I've just had Jason on the phone. He said you'd done one with some bloke in a car."

"A friend, Elwyn, that's all. We're having coffee and a chat to try and clear my head."

She rang off. *Coffee and a chat.* No way would Elwyn swallow that. Not given the state she was in.

"My people can't find Franklin," she told Jed. "They've tried everywhere."

"I know somewhere he might be, a place not many folk know about. Anyone who moves in Franklin's world or has done his research will know about it. It's his special place, he does a lot of business there," Jed nodded knowingly. "He took me there once. He was showing off, wanted me to see his then pride and joy."

"And that is?"

"A car, an old sports job from the sixties. Franklin has been doing it up for years. He has it stashed in a unit on one of his industrial estates."

It was worth a try. After all, they had nothing else.

CHAPTER FIFTY-TWO

Elwyn and Jonny stood at the door to Alice Brough's house. She answered their knock immediately and let them in.

"I presume the visit is because I saw a colleague of yours earlier today," she said. "I knew you'd be round. You people are so predictable."

Elwyn couldn't fault her logic. He shrugged. "We'd like to know what you were doing at Hugo Franklin's house."

"And if I don't want to tell you?" She smirked. "It isn't any of your business. I can go where I like, I don't have to explain myself to you."

Elwyn was not in any mood to play games. "Mia King is missing," he said. "We believe she's been abducted, and Franklin may be able to help us. We need your help to find him, Ms Brough."

"I see. And if I don't know where he is?"

Elwyn couldn't understand why she was being so cagey. "If you know anything about the man, or where he might be, I urge you to tell us."

"What do you want with him? I understand the panic about Mia but what's Hugo Franklin got to do with it? He didn't take her."

"We think he can tell us who might have."

"Why would he? From what little I know of him, he doesn't go around abducting people. He's a businessman, a developer."

Elwyn was getting angry. It was a simple enough question. "We need to ask him something that will help the case we're working on. That, in turn, will help us find Mia."

"You mean Oliver's murder? That case?"

"Yes! Please, Alice," Elwyn asked, "if you know where he is, just tell us."

"I can't help you. Apart from which, I have no interest in finding Oliver's killer. Good luck to him, that's what I say. He was a bastard."

"Alice, we'll arrest you for obstruction if you don't help us." Elwyn was losing it.

He'd touched a nerve. She heaved a deep sigh and reached for a pile of paperwork sitting on the table. "Hugo Franklin can help me with this." She held up her twin brother's birth certificate. "You know how important it is for me to find my twin, Alfie."

"How can Franklin help?" Elwyn was mystified.

"Because I know who Franklin really is. I told you when you first came here. I've done my research." She gave him a sly look. "You should try it for yourself, instead of bothering me."

"Who is he, Alice?" Jonny asked.

"He's my father's older brother, my uncle. His real name is Hugo Brough. They went their separate ways years ago. Don't ask me why, because I have no idea. But I do know this much. My dad hates him. I've never seen such venom. Whatever happened between the two of them was so traumatic that it split the family apart. Both Uncle Hugo and my dad went into care until Aunt Hettie took my dad on."

"Why should we believe you?" asked Jonny.

"Because it's the truth. Check the records, it's simple enough. Here, look at this."

Alice passed them a sheaf of old photos, showing two boys at various stages of growing up. In the last one they were in their early teens. One was dark and tall for his age, but it was the other one that had their attention. A lad with curly blond hair and fine features.

"Remind you of anyone?" Elwyn asked Jonny. He was thinking about Oliver Frodsham and Luke Shaw. "When did you last see your father?" he asked Alice.

"First Hugo and now my dad. Jesus! I've no idea. He's a grown-up, he does what he wants."

"Just answer the question, Alice," Elwyn said, trying to keep calm.

"He's back from his business trip. He was in the garden earlier, doing what he always does, messing around with his roses." She sniffed. "Those bloody flowers get more attention than me."

"Is he still there?" Jonny asked.

"He went out about an hour ago, said he had something to do and hasn't returned. I've tried ringing him but no joy, I'm afraid."

"Did he take his car?" Elwyn asked.

She nodded. "It's a red Citroen. I'll get you the registration number."

Jonny went to the French windows and stared out at the huge garden. "There's smoke coming from over there." He pointed over to a corner half-hidden behind some shrubs.

"That'll be the weeds and grass clippings in the incinerator," Alice said. "It's okay, it's a huge thing. It'll burn away all day. He gets rid of all the garden rubbish that way."

Jonny walked out onto the patio. "There's a funny smell out here."

"He uses a lot of pesticide and stuff."

"Do you mind if I take a look?" Elwyn asked her.

"Help yourself, but don't touch anything. My dad's very possessive about his garden."

* * *

The expanse of land at the rear of house was large and mostly flat. Alexander Brough had created a landscape of shrubs and paths, and taking pride of place in a south facing bed was a huge rose garden. Elwyn followed a path which wandered around behind a high privet hedge, and came across a brick outbuilding hidden out of sight of the house. The incinerator Alice had mentioned was beside it and was emitting a black, acrid smoke. Surely grass clippings didn't burn like that?

He tried to lift the lid and take a look but the thing was too hot to touch. Instead, he ventured towards the open door of the building. It was cool inside, almost icy, a skylight providing what little natural light there was. Shelving around the walls held pots and other gardening paraphernalia, but what took Elwyn's attention was a heap of something lying in the centre of the floor, covered by a tarpaulin.

He shivered. Something wasn't right. He couldn't say what, but it made the hairs on the back of his neck stand on end. He lifted a corner of the tarpaulin and shrank back in disgust and horror. What lay underneath was one of the most appalling things he'd ever seen — the dismembered and charred body of a man. The head, balanced on the burnt torso, was untouched and the eyes, so it seemed to Elwyn, were full of terror. From the photographs he'd seen, Elwyn was in no doubt. He'd found Hugo Franklin.

CHAPTER FIFTY-THREE

Jed McAteer drove Rachel in silence, taking the dual carriageway towards the city centre. Several miles further on, he turned off for Didsbury but bypassed the village, instead taking a road that led towards Chorlton.

"Keep your eyes peeled. It's called 'Franklin Industrial,'" he said.

"I thought you knew where this place was," Rachel replied.

"It's a few years since I came here last. The area has changed since then."

Due to the activities of Franklin's company no doubt. "There! That sign, it's pointing down that lane, to the left."

The industrial estate was small, no more than half a dozen units. Jed parked up in front of the largest detached unit at the far end of the row. "This is it."

"There's no car. He can't be here either." Rachel was beginning to think they'd never find Franklin. Perhaps the killer had got to him too. Or alternatively, he was part of the whole thing and had done a runner.

Jed got out of the car and scouted around the unit, rattling the doors and peering through the one grimy window.

"See anything?" Rachel said. "I'll go round the back."

She left him examining the lock. There was nothing at the rear of the workshop but another mud-splattered window. This was a waste of time. Soul-destroying. Where was Franklin, and where was her girl? They were getting nowhere.

"Rachel, I'm in!"

Rachel rushed back to find Jed. She'd no idea how he'd managed to get inside so fast.

"Someone has been here before us," he said. "The lock has been drilled out and snapped off. From the bits of metal lying around, I'd say it was done recently."

"There's no old car in here," she exclaimed. "It's full of rubbish, just boxes and bits of old furniture."

"Like I said, the car project was a while ago. Have a look around. We're in now, we might as well make sure."

"You think Mia might be here? We have no reason to suspect Franklin, you know. We simply want to talk to him," she said.

"You don't know who you're dealing with," Jed said.

"Why are you so down on Franklin? Is it because he's your rival in the building trade?"

He laughed. "No, but he's a rival in my other 'business.' Look around you. Use that copper's brain of yours," he tapped her head. "What do you see?"

Rachel's heart was hammering again. What other business? The place was nothing but a mess, a dumping ground. But for what?

"Franklin has been in the building business for less than ten years. Look at what he's achieved in such a short time. That takes money, Rachel. A whole lot of money. Where do you think it came from?"

"I've no idea."

Jed pulled one of the boxes across the floor. "Look at this. Tell me, what do you imagine that white powder is?"

The box was empty but there was a residue of powder in the bottom. "You're saying that Franklin is into drug dealing?" Rachel was shocked. "You have to be wrong. We had no idea. Not even the drugs squad are aware of this."

"You and your colleagues don't move in the same circles as me. Let's leave it at that for now."

"But there is precious little security here. You broke that lock in seconds. With that little lot hanging about, it should be like Fort Knox!"

"The lock had already been broken. Franklin's people come here to drop off and pick up only. I bet the stuff is delivered and is gone within the hour. For the purposes of the drop-off Franklin will bring his muscle along. The industrial estate is empty and in the middle of nowhere. For the rest of the time, no one is interested."

"Did you know what went on here?"

"I've been here before. I suspected Franklin was up to something, so I had him watched. I thought I'd use what I knew to my advantage. The units on this site are empty apart from this one. I offered to buy the land but he refused to sell. I tried to pressure him but it didn't work. I have stuff on him, but that sort of thing works both ways. In the end, I backed off."

"I'll have to report this," she said.

"Not yet. We need to find Mia first."

Rachel looked around. There were dozens of boxes. A lot of cocaine. There was no way she could let this go.

"I have to report this." Her voice was weary.

"Drop it, Rachel. We've got more important things to worry about right now."

Reporting the find and admitting what she knew meant owning up to knowing Jed. But should she even care? Rachel was fed up with wrestling with the rights and wrongs of the job. All she wanted was to find Mia. After that, she might never go back to work again.

Jed was getting impatient. He was shifting stuff around, throwing empty cardboard containers across the floor, getting nowhere.

Her mobile beeped. It was Elwyn.

"Rachel, we've found Franklin," he said. "I'm sorry, but he's dead. No help there, I'm afraid. It looks like Alexander Brough killed him. We found him in the Broughs' garden."

It made no sense. Alex Brough was practically a neighbour. He was Alice's dad. Why would he kill someone? "I don't understand. You must have this wrong."

"Brough was Franklin's brother. According to Alice, he hated Hugo Franklin."

"Have you got him?"

"No. He left here an hour ago. Alice has no idea where he's gone, and he isn't answering his mobile. He's driving a red Citroen. Rachel, I think he killed the others too. Alice showed me a photo. When Franklin was younger he looked scarily like Frodsham and Shaw. What's more, Franklin's body has been partially burned."

They'd done it, finally cracked the case. But Rachel took no pleasure in their success. Her head was swimming, and she leaned against the wall to stop herself from falling. Brough had to be found, and they had to make him talk. He was the only person who knew where Mia was.

"You have to find him. He's our last chance of finding my girl."

She stood where she was for a few moments, watching Jed. What to tell him?

"Franklin's dead," she began. "This man I know killed him. My team think he killed the others too."

"Have they got him?" Jed asked.

"No. And we've no idea where he's gone. All we know is that he went out in his car, a red one."

Jed picked up a box and hurled it across the room. Rachel winced. He was so volatile, so full of rage.

"This is hopeless. I'll take you back." He made for the door. "Get in the car." he growled.

She watched him pull the garage doors shut and take a last look at the other units.

He started the engine and sat looking at her. "Well? Any ideas?"

"No. I just want her back."

CHAPTER FIFTY-FOUR

For the first time in years, Alex Brough was truly happy. It was like all his Christmases had come at once. All the practice, all the planning, and even the mistakes had been worth it. He was finally free of his brother and no one was any the wiser.

By the time he'd finished with him, Hugo was a jabbering wreck. Bloodied and battered, he'd pleaded for his life. He'd even wept. Finally, he'd been able to truly terrify the man who all his life had terrified him. It gladdened his heart.

Now there was the cleaning up to do. He had already dismembered Hugo and would continue to burn him bit by bit over the coming days. What was left after that would become fertiliser for his roses. Disposing of Hugo wasn't a problem. It was the girl who was the worry. Sad as it was, she had to go. She knew who he was now. Let her go and she'd tell that nosey mother of hers, and he'd be locked up. He might have a terminal illness, but Brough wanted to spend what little time was left to him in enjoying his garden, and particularly his roses. He couldn't let a slip of a girl ruin his precious freedom.

Mia King had served her purpose. If things had got tricky, if the police had come calling, he would have made use of her, held her to ransom in return for his freedom. But that wasn't necessary now. He was free and clear.

He'd put her somewhere she was unlikely to be found, but there was always that small chance. Hugo had no more use for his workshop, so he would torch it — get rid of all the evidence.

* * *

"Surely there's something else we can do?" Rachel asked as they headed back towards the main road.

"Get real, Rachel. We have no idea what that lunatic has done with her," Jed said.

Rachel dabbed at her eyes. "We can't just give up. What if we don't find Brough?"

Jed wasn't listening. He slowed down and pulled onto the grass verge. "Are you watching the traffic?"

"No. Why?"

"This is a back road that eventually leads to the motorway but one has just turned off onto the track that leads to the industrial estate."

"Was it red?"

"I didn't notice, but there's nowhere else it could be going. It certainly wasn't big enough for a drugs delivery."

"It has to be Brough! But why come here?"

Jed looked at her, and said, "Mia." He swung the car around and headed back. "If he's hurt her, I'll kill the bastard!"

Rachel wasn't listening, she was on her mobile, ringing Elwyn. "Franklin Industrial estate in Chorlton. We've just spotted Brough on his way there. We think that's where he's holding Mia. I need backup and an ambulance here, pronto."

"The ambulance perhaps, but why the troops, Rachel?" Jed shouted at her. "I'm perfectly capable of dealing with Brough."

"You're not touching him," she said. "You have to leave this to me now."

"In your dreams! No one takes my child like that and gets away with it."

He pulled up in front of the garage. The doors were swinging open. Jed leapt out of the car and ran inside. By the time she got out, he'd reappeared with Brough in a headlock.

"The bastard had a can of petrol. He was about to torch the place with Mia still in it. Where's your handcuffs? I need something to restrain him."

Before Rachel could even think, Jed had spun Brough round and punched him full in the face, knocking him to the ground.

Jed looked down at him and spat. "That should keep him quiet."

"Oh, great! Now he won't tell us a thing. How do we find Mia with him out of it?"

Jed went into the building, returned with a length of rope and proceeded to tie Brough's hands behind his back. Then he gave him a brutal kicking.

"Stop it!" Rachel screamed at him. "You're not getting us anywhere like that."

"Perhaps not, but it makes me feel a helluva lot better." He took a deep breath. "Now we find Mia."

"But we know there's nothing in there, we've just come from the place! It's just another storage facility."

"But now we know that Mia has to be here. Why else would he return? It's a garage. Franklin did up his car in here. He was always working on the engine. He never had a ramp, so he must have had a pit."

"A pit? What do you mean?"

"A hole in the ground to stand in so you can work on a vehicle from underneath. Most garages have them."

Rachel shivered. "You mean he's put my girl in a hole in the ground? How are we going to find it?"

"Shift these boxes out of the way. There'll be a cover on the floor somewhere. It'll have a handle to pull it open."

Rachel wondered how long they'd been here. Elwyn should arrive any moment now. She didn't want him to see

Jed, but what choice did she have? Without his help, she'd never have got this far.

"Found it!" Jed shouted.

He took hold of a ring-pull type handle and yanked on it. "Light!" he yelled.

Rachel found the main switch on the wall and turned the electricity on. The place lit up, including a light inside the pit. And there, curled up and still, lay Mia.

"Is she . . ?" Rachel stared down at her child. Why wasn't she moving?

"No. I expect he drugged her."

Jed got down into the pit and lifted her carefully out. He laid her on the ground and then leapt out himself. "Where's that ambulance?"

Rachel took off her jacket and put it over Mia. The girl was cold. She felt her pulse. It was faint. "Ring them again," she said.

Ignoring her, Jed picked up Mia and went outside, making for his car. "It'll be quicker to take her ourselves."

"I can't just leave Brough here on his own. He might escape."

She heard a car. Elwyn was pulling up. "We've got her!" she called. "We're taking her to hospital, Oxford Road in Manchester. She's alright but needs attention."

But Elwyn was staring at Jed. "Glad she's safe, but what's *he* doing here?"

"It's a long story. I'll tell you later. We need to go."

They sped away leaving Elwyn, no doubt, with a shedload of questions. Rachel thought only of her daughter. Right now, nothing else mattered.

CHAPTER FIFTY-FIVE

Two days later

Superintendent Harding was addressing the team. "He won't stop talking. Alex Brough is not in the least sorry for what he did. Had you not stepped in when you did, Franklin would have ended up as fertiliser for roses. Brough's only regret is having been caught. He claims to be terminally ill and hoped to spend his last months in his garden."

Amy nudged Jonny. "Obviously a psycho," she whispered.

"Who? Harding or Brough?" He grinned.

"DCI King will be back tomorrow. I'm told her daughter is on the mend." He cleared his throat. "You all did well," he said. It sounded grudging. "It was a good outcome." He turned on his heel and left.

"There is stuff I don't get, though." Jonny turned to Elwyn. "How did the boss know where her daughter was, and who helped her with Brough? She didn't knock him about like that on her own."

Elwyn looked up from his desk. "There are some things about this case, DC Farrell, that you may never be privy to. If I were you, I'd leave it at that."

"Something juicy, I bet," Amy whispered. "Elwyn's not been right since. Did you read the report? How was Jed McAteer involved? What did he have to do with it?"

Elwyn had overheard. "He was put out at being implicated in Greyson's murder, and he'd been hounding Rachel for an apology." Elwyn didn't know if that was the truth or not, but it was the only explanation that made any sense to him. "McAteer told Rachel that Franklin was a villain, and not the super clean businessman we all thought he was. He knew about Franklin's drug dealing, and the garage, and he took Rachel there. That was a real tough day for her. All she wanted was her daughter back, and she would have accepted help from the Devil if he'd offered. Thankfully, it ended well."

"So it was McAteer who beat up Brough. Why?"

"How do I know?" Elwyn said. He too had questions about that day. He needed a word with Rachel. "Any more loose ends?" he asked Amy and Jonny.

Jonny shrugged. "Can't think of any. We know Franklin went to Brough's house after he left his office. We found his car in the track at the back of the Broughs' garden. And, of course, we now know the two of them were brothers. Brough hated Franklin because of the brutal bullying he'd subjected him to when they were kids."

"Makes you think, doesn't it?" Amy shuddered. "I'm not very nice to my brother at times. Perhaps I should try harder."

"Brough will get what's coming to him. Apart from his confession, we've got plenty of evidence — Franklin's body for one, and forensics found his prints on the Kings' doorbell and in Croft's house."

"He'll go away for a long time." Jonny nodded to Amy.

"Right," Elwyn announced. "I'm off out for a while. Man the phones and get those reports finished. I'll be back in an hour or so."

* * *

"Elwyn! What a nice surprise," Rachel said. "Come in. I'll get you a brew."

He stood on the doorstep, hesitant. "I'm not sure if this is a social call or not."

"Problem?"

"It's the McAteer thing. You may have convinced Harding and the team, but not me. There are things that don't add up. Has McAteer been hassling you?"

Rachel laughed. "No. In the end he helped me. I wouldn't have got Mia back without him."

Elwyn didn't look convinced. "I thought he might be the reason you were so preoccupied these last few days. Officially, McAteer was pissed off at being implicated in Greyson's murder, but we both know he wouldn't give a damn about that. It'd be water off a duck's back. McAteer gets the blame for lots of things and lets it go."

She laughed that one off too, although not very convincingly. "Come on, Elwyn, what could McAteer be hassling me about?"

"He came here, didn't he? It was his car you got into when Jason was doing the forensic search. You nipped off with him pretty quick then."

Rachel sighed. Elwyn was a stickler for detail. He would dig and dig, and finally worm his way to the truth. "Please, Elwyn. Just drop it."

"I can't. He's a villain. He's involved in big-time crime in this city, and well you know it. So why accept his help without telling us first?"

"I had no choice. I had to get Mia back."

"What made you think McAteer knew where she was?"

"He didn't. But he knew Franklin, and he knew about the unit and what was kept there. It was a hunch, that's all."

"I still don't get it." He shook his head. "How could he turn up like that, just in time to save the day?"

Elwyn was looking her straight in the eye. Here it came. She knew Elwyn. He'd have saved the best until last.

"How did he even know Mia was missing? We hadn't made any announcements. We'd only just found out ourselves."

She'd had it. The strain of these last few days had left her drained and unable to think straight. Rachel clenched her fists and closed her eyes.

She didn't want to see Elwyn's face when she said this.

"He knew because I told him." The silence pounded inside her head. "I had no choice. I had to make sure she wasn't with him." She opened her eyes and looked right back at him. "Jed McAteer is Mia's father."

Elwyn's face gave no hint of what he was thinking. Rachel busied herself making the tea, the clatter of mugs drowning out the uneasy silence. She wanted him to say something, shout, anything. His silence was unbearable.

"Here." She handed him a mug.

"Why didn't you tell me?"

"Why do you think? I tell you about my relationship with Jed, and it puts our working relationship in jeopardy."

"I'm not that petty, Rachel. What did you think I'd do — go running to Harding? Tell tales?"

"I'm a DCI for God's sake. If Jed is ever involved in a crime we're investigating, it will make things tricky. I might have to take the flak, but I wanted to spare you."

"No need. I'm a big boy now."

Rachel watched him sip at his tea. "What are you going to do?"

"Nothing. I certainly won't tell anyone else. This is your mess, and I'm happy for it to stay that way." He paused, helping himself to a biscuit from the tin. "But now I understand, and everything falls into place. That's all I needed." He smiled.

Rachel didn't know how to take that. "Okay. Anything cracks off with Jed in the future and we behave as normal. No special treatment for him or me."

"Agreed."

"What's Brough said?" she asked, changing the subject.

"Too much. Some of the detail was sickening. And he's confessed, so there'll be no protracted trial."

That was a relief.

"I heard from Jason earlier," she said. "I'd asked him to find out if Alice Brough had a twin. I wanted him to check the hospital records for me. He did, and she's been telling the truth all along. She did have a twin brother. He was called Alfie Brough."

"So, what happened to him?"

"I've no idea," Rachel replied. "Someone might ask Brough."

"Why would he tell us?"

"You say he's confessed to everything else. It is quite possible that he killed his son and wife as well."

Elwyn nodded. "You could be right. But where are they?"

"You have no hunches?"

She knew the look. Elwyn had an idea. "What is it?" she asked.

"Something Harding said this morning about Brough's rose garden. That's where Brough was going to put his brother."

"It's worth a try. Do you want to ring Jason, or should I?"

"Does this mean you're back?" He smiled.

"No reason not to put my toe in the water. Providing you are okay with it, given my revelation about McAteer."

He gave her a sideways glance. "Get your coat. We'll go and speak to Alice."

* * *

Alice Brough didn't seem surprised to see them. "You want to search the place again?"

"No, Alice. This is about your brother and mother. We've checked out your story and now we know that you did have a twin. What bothers us is what happened to him."

"It's bothered me for years, but no one has ever taken any notice." She sighed. "Help yourselves. But there's not an inch of this place your people haven't already turned over."

"What about the rose garden?" Elwyn asked.

Alice was silent, a strange look in her eyes. "They didn't do any digging. But my dad would go out there and he'd be talking to himself. Weird, but I never queried it. I'd heard that some people reckon that talking to your plants makes them grow better."

"Our forensic people will bring some equipment and have a look. But they'll have to do quite a bit of digging."

"Do what you like. I hate the bloody roses anyway. He spent most of his free time out there. Barely spoke to me."

"How are you doing, Alice?" Rachel asked gently. "It can't be easy. You're alone now and this house has some bad memories for you."

"You think I can't hack it?" She stood with her hands on her hips, defiant. "I'll be fine. I'm back at college next week. Tell Megan I'll ring her."

"I will, but if you need to talk to someone, we can arrange it."

"I'll keep it in mind. But I can't get away from the fact that my dad's insane, a serial killer. I doubt I'll want to talk about that one for some time."

"A counsellor would be happy to listen to whatever you tell them. It doesn't have to be about your dad. Don't shut people out, Alice."

"I'm sure I'll be fine, Mrs King. This house is paid for and there's money enough in the bank. I'm a tough cookie. Please don't waste your time worrying about me."

EPILOGUE

Two days later

"Bones under the roses? That's just gross!" Amy declared.

"Two skeletons buried in the garden," Rachel told the team. "Tests are still ongoing but from their sizes, we think they are Julia and Alfie Brough."

"I asked him," Elwyn said. "He laughed at me. Said they were better off without his wife. According to him, she irritated him beyond measure. Her mood went up and down and she used to hide away for days on end. During her periods of depression the kids went without food and rarely went to school."

Rachel frowned. "That's no reason to kill her. Jason said Julia had numerous broken bones and both had skull fractures. It could have happened post-mortem, but we'll never know now."

"Any evidence of burning?" Jonny asked.

"Not that Jason can tell."

"He insists he didn't kill his son, says that was down to Julia. He says that one day in a fit of rage, she hit the child. Alfie fell and banged his head. Brough was distraught and so was she. That was when he lost it and killed her," Rachel said.

"Not that convincing," Elwyn said.

It had been a difficult case. Despite the timescale and the different methods of killing, one man had been responsible for all the deaths. A surprising outcome. If, at the start of it, she'd had to pin the killings on anyone, even though she hardly knew him, Rachel would never have chosen Alex Brough.

Rachel went back to her office, Elwyn following her. "Celebration?" he asked.

"Okay. We'll have a quick one in the pub later. I'll buy."

"Heard from your friend?" Elwyn closed the door.

"He's visited Mia a couple of times. He's been very reasonable, and agreed not to say anything to Alan for the time-being." She rolled her eyes. "But I'm not daft. He'll drop that bombshell in time, when it suits him."

"Then what?"

"Alan will be devastated. After all, he did bring her up. I'll try and make Jed see sense, but it will need a lot of negotiation and that's what bothers me. Do you know? He'd been seeing Mia for weeks and I knew nothing about it! He was very cautious, and always made sure she took a friend with her. He took her shopping round the Trafford Centre last month, and I never even noticed the new clothes. What sort of mother does that make me?"

"A busy one. Don't beat yourself up."

"It's tricky though, isn't it? Jed will want in and Mia likes him a lot. She's not daft, the questions will come soon enough."

"Explaining how you got involved with one of Manchester's most notorious villains is the biggy."

She sniffed. "He wasn't a villain when we first met. We were both students."

"Can't imagine you as a student." He smiled.

Rachel picked up the cushion from her chair and threw it at him. "Bring that stuff of yours round to ours later, if you want. I'll make us some supper. I never asked — where are you living?"

"I've got a room at my sister's. But it's not ideal and she wants rid of me, so I'm looking for somewhere. Marie has agreed that we sell the house and split the proceeds."

"If you get really stuck, there's always mine. I'll stick one of the girls next door with Alan."

"I hope that villain never embarrasses you, Rachel. You could go far career wise, but not dragging McAteer's shadow behind you."

Rachel looked at him and shook her head. "Do you think I don't know that, Elwyn? I just have to hope that he has the good grace to keep off my patch." She folded her arms and gave him a small smile. "On the plus side, he'll make a damn good informant. Look at what he gave us about Franklin and the drugs. Never seen the drug squad boss so happy."

"I take it you're no longer thinking of ditching the job?"

"No. For now I'm fine with things as they are. The jitters were because of Jed and the possibility of having to deal with him, and explain it all to you."

"You don't have to worry about me, Rachel. We stick together. Never forget that." With that, Elwyn left her to it.

Rachel was really grateful that Elwyn had taken her involvement with Jed so well. It could so easily have gone the other way. But with that knowledge came future problems that she could only guess at. She flopped down in her chair. There was a mountain of paperwork on her desk and not much time.

"Head down, girl," she said to herself.

THE END

ALSO BY HELEN H. DURRANT

THE DETECTIVE RACHEL KING BOOKS
Book 1: *Next Victim*
Book 2: *Two Victims*
Book 3: *Wrong Victim*
Book 4: *Forgotten Victim*

THE DCI GRECO BOOKS
Book 1: *Dark Murder*
Book 2: *Dark Houses*
Book 3: *Dark Trade*
Book 4: *Dark Angel*

THE CALLADINE & BAYLISS MYSTERY SERIES
Book 1: *Dead Wrong*
Book 2: *Dead Silent*
Book 3: *Dead List*
Book 4: *Dead Lost*
Book 5: *Dead & Buried*
Book 6: *Dead Nasty*
Book 7: *Dead Jealous*
Book 8: *Dead Bad*
Book 9: *Dead Guilty*
Book 10: *Dead Wicked*

MATT BRINDLE
Book 1: *His Third Victim*
Book 2: *The Other Victim*

DETECTIVES LENNOX & WILDE
Book 1: *The Guilty Man*
Book 2: *The Faceless Man*

Thank you for reading this book.

If you enjoyed it please leave feedback on Amazon or Goodreads, and if there is anything we missed or you have a question about, then please get in touch. We appreciate you choosing our book.

Founded in 2014 in Shoreditch, London, we at Joffe Books pride ourselves on our history of innovative publishing. We were thrilled to be shortlisted for Independent Publisher of the Year at the British Book Awards.

www.joffebooks.com

Join our mailing list to be the first to hear about Helen H. Durrant's next mystery, coming soon!